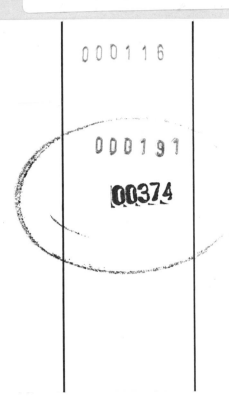

The Adventures of King Midas

Lynne Reid Banks
Illustrated by Hilda Offen

Collins

An imprint of HarperCollinsPublishers

For E.

First published in Great Britain by HarperCollins in 1993
First published in paperback in Young Lions in 1993
This edition published in Collins in 1998
Collins is an imprint of HarperCollins*Publishers* Ltd
77-85 Fulham Palace Road, Hammersmith,
London, W6 8JB

1 3 5 7 9 8 6 4 2

Text copyright © Lynne Reid Banks 1993
Illustrations copyright © Hilda Offen 1993

ISBN 0 00 674728 0

The author and illustrator assert the moral right to
be identified as the author and illustrator of the work.

Printed and bound in Great Britain by
Caledonian International Book Manufacturing Ltd,
Glasgow G64

Chapter One

The Wish

King Midas was nothing special, as kings go. He hadn't got a particularly large kingdom, just a small one, and it wasn't either rich or poor. Just ordinary, really. Like the King himself, until a certain day in his life, on which everything changed.

But until that day, things jogged along for him quite normally. Of course, you might not think it normal to live in a small but charming palace surrounded by beautiful grounds, to have to sign papers all the time, wear a heavy crown quite often, and to have dozens of servants running around to do your bidding. But that's normal for a king, and King Midas was quite used to it and thought nothing of it.

He hadn't got a queen.

He'd had one, once, but sadly, she'd died. The King was terribly grieved. She had been so

5

beautiful – a shining golden beauty that made the sun and the stars come out for him. He kept a lock of her hair, the colour of summer pollen, in a locket round his neck, and would take it out and smooth it in his fingers to keep it shiny and alive-looking.

But he had something better than that left from his happy younger days: a little daughter called Delia.

She looked rather like her mother – the same bright brown eyes and sun-spun golden hair, and lively, loving ways. King Midas simply adored her, and made a great fuss of her, giving her most of what she asked for and thinking of all kinds of lovely surprises for her.

But oddly enough, she wasn't spoilt. She went to school in the village near the palace, like other children, and was quite ordinary, too, in a way. Of course, a princess can never be entirely ordinary, but there was one nice thing about her – she never boasted or gave herself airs. She was a very nice girl, really, which made what happened to her all the worse. She simply didn't deserve it.

As to whether the King deserved to be the cause of this awful thing that happened to his beloved child, that's another matter. There's no denying that he had a fault. Who hasn't? But this one was bad enough to lead him into the most dire trouble.

He allowed to grow in him a great desire, which came to rule his whole life.

He thought nobody knew about it. But little

things gave him away to those quick-witted enough to understand.

For instance, one day some large oil paintings that he'd ordered from abroad arrived in big flat packing-cases. He was very excited and as soon as they were unpacked, he called Delia.

"You must see my new paintings, my darling," he cried cheerfully. "You've got such an eye, I can't wait to hear what you think of them!"

Delia had no more "eye" than most people, but she did like paintings. She loved making up stories about them. So she hurried after her father to one of the long galleries in the palace.

"I must supervise the hanging," said the King importantly.

"Daddy, you know you've done away with capital punishment!" teased Delia.

The King laughed uproariously. He was in a very good mood.

There were already several servants up ladders, and several more below, with the first great canvas in their hands, ready to hand it up to those above. The King, who had arrived beaming with pleasure, took one look at the picture and flew into one of his rare, but alarming, rages.

"Take them away!" he roared. "I won't have them! I don't want them – *not like that!*"

One of his personal servants called Biffpot, the only one who dared speak to him when he was angry, murmured, "But Sire, the paintings are very fine!"

"The paintings? The PAINTINGS? Who's

talking about the *paintings*? It's the FRAMES I can't abide! GET THOSE FRAMES OUT OF MY SIGHT!"

"But Daddy, what's wrong with the frames?" Delia exclaimed anxiously. "They're beautiful, all carved and gilded –"

"Gilded! Precisely, my darling! You have put your finger on it! They are gilded! I would rather, far rather, have plain wooden ones than these – these – these pretenders! I tell you I will not be lied to – *not even by a picture frame!*"

And he stormed away, leaving the servants agape and Delia close to tears.

Later, in the servants' hall, there was much gossip, and not for the first time.

"The King's got this *thing* about fakes," the butler remarked knowingly. "What they call a *fixation*."

"No," said the manservant who had been trying to hang up the picture. "He's got a thing about *lies*. And I believe it's called an *obsession*."

But Biffpot, who was closer to the King than the others, being his personal valet, shook his head sadly.

"His Majesty," he said, "is indeed obsessed AND fixated. But not with the things you mentioned. It is much, much more serious than that."

"So what is it?" asked the others. But Biffpot only shook his head in a worried way and wouldn't answer directly.

"I will say only this," he said. "It is one of the

most serious obsessions anyone can have, and No Good Will Come Of It."

How right he was.

So Biffpot knew about the King's desire. And soon, one other person knew, because Midas told her – Delia.

When she was at school, and he had finished his signing for the day and had nothing much to distract him, he would walk about the palace and the gardens, with his hands behind his back and his head down on his chest, feeling deeply depressed. No, it was more like feeling desperately hungry. Only what he was hungry for wasn't food.

Once, Delia, returning from school and not finding him in his office, came out to look for him in the garden. She saw him at a distance and crept up behind him, but when, startled out of his dream, he turned suddenly, she saw he had tears on his face.

She threw herself into his arms.

"Daddy! You're crying! What's wrong, were you thinking of Mother?"

"Ah, my darling! If it were only that! I wish I could say I had been, but no. I'll tell you the truth, but promise you won't tell."

"Of course, I'd never tell your secrets," she said, snuggling under his arm. "It can't be anything bad."

He found it very difficult to explain. He cleared his throat several times, and then said:

"Have you ever looked around you, and wished everything were a different colour?"

She stared at him. "No."

He tried again.

"Have you ever thought how wonderful it would be, if everything were made of – a different kind of stuff?"

"No . . . What kind of stuff?"

"Well, er – anything you like. Chocolate, perhaps?"

She wrinkled up her nose and shook her head. "Too sticky."

"Wouldn't you like it if everything around us were a toy, something for you to play with?"

"But then nothing would be real and there'd be no point in pretending."

He groaned, and came right out with it.

"Well, wouldn't you think it was the most wonderful thing in the world *if everything were made of gold?*"

She gazed at him open-mouthed. "I think that would be horrid," she said. Then she saw his face fall. "Oh, Daddy! I'm sorry, is that what *you* want?"

He nodded, and she saw the hungry, haunted look in his eyes. She didn't know what to say. She felt quite shocked and upset. It seemed so . . . But she couldn't think words like "silly" and "greedy" about her father.

"But Daddy," she said slowly. "We've got so much gold already. More than most people at school will ever see in their whole lives."

He said nothing.

"We've got all that gold jewellery of Mother's, and your gold watch, and the gold ornaments, and the special gold knives and forks and plates for state dinners, and –"

But the King was shaking his head.

"It's – it's not enough, somehow," he muttered.

"But if it's *money* you want, we've got the Treasury!"

"They send me what I order in –" (he shuddered) "*bank notes,*" he said with disgust. "Dirty, deceitful things, pretending to be gold, well, as good as gold, but they're lying, *they're lying!*" His round, jolly face went dark red, and Delia backed away a step. He quickly controlled himself and reached out his hand to her. It was trembling.

"Delia . . . Tell me it's not madness. Tell me you understand."

She couldn't. So she just held his hand tight and looked at the ground. They stood like that for a moment. Then she raised her face.

"You'll get over it, Daddy. Now please, stop grumping around and come and read my new book with me!"

And she tugged him after her.

The King shook himself free of his longing, for the moment, and tried to cheer up for Delia's sake, because he loved her. But the thing was getting too strong for him. It seemed to be taking him over. Any time he wasn't busy, or was feeling a bit down, that gnawing hunger would come back to him, and he would just have to go away by himself and wish and wish and wish for gold.

One day, when he was feeling like this and walking about the garden, he was startled to see a little old man – really little, about two feet tall – with a long white beard and a black cloak, pop out from behind a bush in front of the King.

Midas blinked. "Good morning," he said politely.

"It isn't good and it isn't morning," snapped the little old man. "It's the middle of the afternoon, as you'd know if you were thinking about it."

"So it is," said the King. "My mind was on something else."

"Obviously."

The King's white moustache (did I mention that he had a white moustache?) began to bristle.

"Excuse me, but who are you, and how did you get into my garden?" he asked.

"My name is Nandan," replied this strange little figure. "I got in by wishing to be in. And speaking of wishes, I see that you have a very powerful one."

Startled, the King said, "What do you mean, you *see*?"

"It's written all over you," replied the little man, his bright eyes twinkling under his bushy eyebrows.

The King looked down at himself. To his amazement, the one word GOLD was written in large letters all over his clothes. Even as he stared, it faded.

"Are you a magician?" he asked in awe.

"Yes, indeed," said Nandan. "A very good one too."

"Can you make a rabbit come out of a hat?" asked the King rather childishly. He had once seen this done, and could never figure out the trick of it.

"Pooh," said Nandan. "Could make an elephant come out of a thimble if I wanted to. Don't want to, though," he said quickly as the King opened his mouth to speak.

"What else can you do?"

"Lots of things," replied the little man.

"Er . . . like what, for instance?" prompted the king, who was dying to see a bit of magic.

For answer, the magician plucked a hair out of his long white beard, flourished it in the air, made a few very dramatic passes at it with his free hand, and turned it into – a dressing-gown cord.

"Oh . . ." exclaimed the king in obvious disappointment.

"What, 'oh'?" asked the little man sharply.

"Bit dull, that's all," muttered the king.

"Pardon me," retorted Nandan sarcastically. "I didn't realise you were so easily bored." And with a brief, dismissive gesture, he tossed the cord away. As it touched the grass, there was a mighty bang, a cloud of smoke, and a huge snake-like monster leapt out of the ground.

Midas fell back in terror as the thing loomed over his head, hissed furiously at him, and then, at another mild gesture from Nandan, disappeared as suddenly as it had come.

Midas found himself on the ground, panting and goggle-eyed. Nandan was examining his fingernails.

"Now, what were we saying?" he remarked.

"That – that was astonishing," the king managed to croak. "Very – ulp! – impressive, I must say."

"What? – Oh, that. Nothing at all, I assure you. Just a little illusion."

Midas felt a perfect idiot. He scrambled to his feet with some difficulty (he was rather fat).

"Shall we get back to your wish?" asked the magician pleasantly.

Midas felt his heart begin to beat strangely. The most incredible notion had come into his head. Could it – could he – might it –? But he couldn't even finish the thought, it was so desperately exciting.

He didn't say anything – just gazed at the magician with a look of longing.

"I could give you that wish, if I wanted to."

"And – and – *do* you want to?" the king got out.

"Might," his visitor answered. "Depends what you'd give me for doing it."

The king swallowed. Even so, he could hardly

articulate. "If you could give me all the g-gold I wanted," he stammered, "I'd give you my best red rose."

Not a lot, you might think, for such a gift. But the King had some sense. He realised that no ordinary, material reward would be any use to a magician of such powers. Nothing but his greatest achievement would suffice.

And the rose *was* his greatest achievement. It was an absolutely new kind, his very own, the product of years of careful work and dedication, recently hailed throughout the rose-growing world and named The Midas. It was said to be the most glorious rose in existence.

Nandan was looking at him with new interest. The old man had the most extraordinary eyes, very bright and twinkly. They reminded Midas of something – he couldn't think what.

"One rose?"

"All of them," Midas said recklessly.

"All of them? For ever? So no one will have a Midas rose but me?"

Midas swallowed again. It meant giving up his one special claim to fame and glory (apart from being a king, which really wasn't his doing). But if he had his wish –! What else mattered?

"All of them, for ever," he said.

The little man gave a tiny, thoughtful nod.

"A bargain," he said.

With a sudden movement he pulled the king's hands towards him and held them tightly by the fingers. Now his eyes were not twinkly any more. They seemed to bore into Midas's brain.

"Listen carefully," he said. "I cannot give you gold. But I can work a spell so that everything your hands touch becomes gold."

The King thought he might lose consciousness. It was too wonderful to be borne.

"Oh, yes!" he said faintly. "Oh, please!"

"Think," said the magician.

"Th-th-think?" the king stammered.

"Yes! Think, man! Think whether you want it or not!"

"I want it! I want it!" cried Midas without thinking for even one second.

"Because the spell is permanent. No way back."

"If I could have this, I would have everything any man could want. It is my one dream of happiness."

"Your dream of happiness! You have your child – you have royal blood – you have the love of your people. You even have wealth. And *this* is your dream of happiness?"

"Do you think it so awful?" asked the King, his hands still firmly held in front of him.

"It is of no importance what I think. Decide."

"I have decided," said the King. "I can't come so close to it and reject it. I want it."

Even as he said these words, he felt a charge, like a bolt of electricity, shoot through his fingers and through his hands, stopping short at his wrists. It shocked him so that he cried out and everything went black for a moment.

When he opened his eyes, things were apparently back to normal. The little man was yawning.

"That's it," he said. "Where's my rose?"

Feeling rather dazed, the king pointed out to him the special rose bush. Not that you could miss it. The roses on it were double the size of any other rose in the garden. They glowed with a special, deep red which seemed to hold all other reds within it. For several yards around the bush the perfume wafted and played in the air, so delicious you could almost see it.

"Ah! Ah!" exclaimed Nandan. "A treasure from the far side of magic! And this is to be mine alone!"

Reverently, he plucked one of the huge roses, attached it to his leather waistcoat, drew in a deep breath of its scent, and gave Midas one long look of – what? Admiration? Gratitude? Whatever it was, Midas felt that for the first time since the magician had appeared, they were equals.

Suddenly the little man made a grasping pass with his hand.

The whole rose bush, covered with Midas roses, vanished.

In another split second, the bush, now a tiny miniature, complete with its roots, reappeared in the little man's hand. He was taking it with him! The Midas rose was no more for this world. The magician gave a high-pitched laugh.

"I've had the best of our bargain," he cried. "Goodbye, King Midas!"

He disappeared into the air, and the roses with him. But after a second, he came back.

"If I were less pleased with my fee, I would not bother to say this," he said. "But if you should ever want to see me again, come to this spot where my rose once grew and say, 'Red Rose, bloom again'. But make sure it's not raining!"

He let out another eldritch chuckle and vanished once more.

Chapter Two

Gold!

*T*he King looked around him.

He wondered if he had been dreaming. He definitely felt dizzy. So he put out his hand and leant against a tree to steady himself.

The rough, warm bark changed instantly under his hand to something hard and smooth and cold. The King took his hand away quickly and looked up at the tree.

At first he couldn't credit what his eyes told him. From its roots to its topmost branches, the tree was made of shining gold. Every tiny leaf was like a golden mirror that shone so brightly it dazzled the King's eyes.

He broke off a leaf and stared at it. He broke off some more, until he had a whole handful. On a sudden impulse, he flung them into the air. Sending out sparks of dancing light, they fell heavily, scattering around his feet.

"It's true," he breathed, gazing at the tree in a befuddlement that trembled on the brink of absolute happiness. "It's TRUE!" he shouted, jumping into the air, grasping a low-hanging golden bough in both hands and swinging on it like a schoolboy. "IT'S TRUE IT'S TRUE IT'S TRUE!" he yelled at the top of his lungs, dropping from the branch and capering around the base of the tree.

"I have it! It's mine! The golden touch is mine!"

He couldn't stay still. He left the heavy shade of the tree and ran to another, and another. Each one froze to his touch into brilliant, solid, flawless gold. The branches stopped swaying and the leaves stopped whispering. The birds that had been resting in the trees flew away in chirping, frightened clouds. Squirrels fled down the trunks, slipping and sliding. Though they couldn't be seen, a myriad of insects also made their escape, or tried to, though many were trapped inside and could no longer gnaw their way out.

But King Midas noticed nothing but that his magic touch worked perfectly, and had already made him the most gold-rich person in the world.

At last he had to stop dashing about. He came, puffing, to rest by a rose bush. Not a Midas bush, of course, that was gone for ever, but a beautiful bush all the same. He was so happy he felt he must pick a rose to put in his button hole; but

as he broke the flower off, the petals became stiff and shiny, and the King found he was holding a perfect golden rose.

His face broke into a grin. "This takes some getting used to!" he exclaimed. And then he did another silly thing. Without thinking, he bent his head to smell the flower.

Of course it had no scent. That had disappeared as soon as the rose became gold.

The King became very still for a moment. Roses were his great love . . . But then he pushed away the tiny regret that had come into his mind. He threw away the golden rose and, with his magic hands firmly out of the way, smelt some others to make himself feel all right again.

The next thing he thought of was some cash that was in his pocket – common coins of the realm, made of copper and bronze and nickel. He would change those into gold at once – gold like the pirates in his old storybooks used to have – doubloons! And he reached into the pocket of his jacket.

Instantly a heavy weight fell onto his shoulders so that he was almost pressed to the ground.

"Good heavens! The *jacket's* turned into gold now! I keep forgetting!"

He had to break the buttons away to get the jacket off, and as it lay all stiff and cold in the grass, gleaming like a suit of armour, the King almost thought for a moment that it had been nicer before.

He shook himself, feeling the chill breeze

without his dear old tweed jacket, his favourite gardening one that he'd had since his wife's time, and exclaimed aloud, "But how absurd! Now I have all the gold I want, I can buy a new jacket for every day of the year! But of course," he added thoughtfully, "I shall have to get someone to dress me. H'm. Wonder what old Biffpot's going to think about all this?"

It was the first time he had considered what anybody else might think, and his thoughts flew to Delia.

"Now she'll see! Now she'll understand!" he thought gleefully, and looked around for something to turn into gold as a special present for her.

In the next section of the garden was a fountain with a statue in the middle of it, of a little girl holding a fish. It was made of marble.

"I'll turn that statue into a golden doll for *my* little girl," he thought. As he reached his hand through the spray to touch the statue, all the drops of water turned into gold too, and fell with little splashes into the pool, where they sank to the bottom and lay among the pebbles.

Somehow this thrilled the King. "It works for *little* things, too!" he thought. "Little, ordinary things!" For pure fun, he touched a stone and saw it glitter among its dull fellows on the path, and then turned a humble garden spade into a magnificent artifact of gold that any museum would give its eye-teeth to own.

"Hooray!" the King cried. "I love this! This is

even more fun than the trees! If that old spade were only alive, how proud it would be in the tool-shed among all the other plain ones!" It was a funny thought, and he laughed aloud.

He was just reaching for the golden statue when a small bird alighted on the rim of the fountain for a drink. It was bright yellow and the king recognised it as one of the palace canaries that must have escaped. Delia was very fond of her birds and the King knew that recapturing this one would please her, so he chirruped to the canary, and held out his finger for the little tame thing to hop onto.

It was clearly tired of being free. Trustingly, it hopped.

Hardly had its feet touched Midas's finger before it fell like a stone into his hand, turned to gold, right to its tipmost wing-feather. It was a very unpleasant feeling, like witnessing sudden death.

The King was dismayed. "Poor little thing!" he cried. "I didn't mean it! – Oh, please come back to life – what will Delia say?"

But the bird lay stiffly in the King's hand and stared at him with its sightless golden eyes.

"I really must be a bit more careful," thought the King. "I can't just go on doing everything the way I did before. Habit. Everything is habit . . . Well, I must break some habits, that's all, it's a small enough price to pay."

He tried to lift the golden statue, but soon realised it would be too heavy for Delia. The touch of it on his fingers gave him a sudden shiver, and he let go of it.

He was feeling hungry as well as chilly; the sun was going down and it was time for supper. He thought about the lovely lamb chops and fruit and cake and red wine that he'd ordered for his meal, and after just touching another thing or two to cheer himself up again, he headed for the palace.

"There's nothing like an afternoon of turning things into gold for giving you an appetite!" he joked to himself, rubbing his magic hands together.

He hurried to the palace dining-room. The first thing he saw as he walked in was a bowl of beautiful fruits on the table. There were apples and pears and peaches and plums, and even a few late figs. Midas licked his lips and imagined his teeth sinking into one of the figs and crunching on the seeds. Or would one of his hot-house peaches be nicer?

Unable to make up his mind, he closed his eyes, picked up a piece of fruit, opened his mouth, and took a big bite.

The next moment the King was shouting and roaring at the top of his voice like an angry lion.

"Ow! Ow!" he bawled, dancing round the dining-room holding his mouth. "I've broken my teeth! I've cracked my jaw! OW!"

A little serving maid came running into the room.

"Your Majesty, whatever's the matter?" she cried in alarm.

"I turned an apple into gold and then hurt my front teeth trying to bite it!" roared the King.

"Oh, surely not, Your Majesty!" said the little maid.

"Are you calling me a liar?" shouted the King, red in the face from pain and rage. And he picked up a pear from the dish and threw it at her.

Luckily it missed, but what it did hit was a large mirror hanging behind her, which it smashed into fragments.

The King stopped roaring at once.

"Seven years' bad luck!" he exclaimed, but the little maid didn't hear him.

"Don't hurt me, Your Majesty!" she cried, hiding her face and running out of the room in tears.

The King stood looking at his broken mirror and almost wanted to cry himself.

"I've frightened that poor child who only wanted to help me," he thought remorsefully, "and I've broken my lovely mirror that's been in the family for years. What a silly old man I am."

But feeling silly didn't stop him from feeling hungry, so when a manservant came in to see what was the matter, he found the King sitting at the table (in a gold chair, which surprised the manservant who was certain all the chairs in the palace were made of wood) holding in his hands a gold knife and fork.

"Who can have laid the table?" thought the servant. "The gold cutlery is only for state banquets!"

Strangest of all, tucked stiffly into the King's shirt front was a cloth-of-gold table-napkin.

"Can I be of any assistance, Sire?" asked the servant, bowing low to hide the look of amazement on his face.

"Yes you can," said the King shortly. "I'm extremely hungry. But I am not able to put any food into my mouth, because everything I touch turns to gold. Even the wine in the goblets! So kindly feed me."

The servant straightened up.

"You say everything Your Majesty touches turns to gold?"

"You're not deaf, are you?" said the King testily.

"Are you sure Your Majesty feels quite well?"

The King knew he was going to get angry again in a minute.

"Of course I'm sure, you fool!" he snapped. "Watch this!"

And he picked up a lamb chop from the plate in front of him.

The manservant's eyes nearly popped out of his head and he made swallowing noises.

"What are you staring at, fellow?" asked the King. "Have you never seen a solid gold lamb chop before?"

"N-no, Sire!" the poor man gasped.

"Well, you have now! Come here at once and

feed me! Or will you stand there and watch your monarch dwindle to skin and bone from lack of nourishment?"

But the man didn't move. At last he finished swallowing and croaked out in a shocked voice: "Forgive me, Sire, but I dare not feed you! You might – you might touch me by mistake, and then I should turn into gold, too!"

"You can't imagine I'd be such an idiot as to touch a living—" The King's eyes fell on the little bird that lay beside his plate, and he stopped shouting suddenly. "H'mph. Harrumph. I promise to be careful." As the man dithered at the far end of the table, the King raised his voice again and shouted: "I said I won't touch you! See! I'm sitting on my hands! Now come here at once and do as you're commanded! Do you think I can't control myself?"

When he still didn't come, the King's patience snapped. He snatched one hand out from under him and banged it on the table.

The gold started from where the King was sitting and went shooting down the length of the long table to the end where the servant stood. He gave a yell, jumped back three feet, knocked into the mantelpiece and tipped a vase full of flowers and cold water over his head.

This broke the poor man's nerve completely.

"Help! Help!" he spluttered, waving his arms. "The King's bewitched!" And he ran wildly from the room.

The King sat and ground his teeth with frustration. Once again he tackled the remains of his dinner with his gold knife and fork, but the magic passed straight through them to the food.

He bent his head to his plate and tried to eat like an animal. But it was hopeless. He couldn't get a proper mouthful.

So he pushed away his useless food and sat alone at his golden table. First he sighed, then he groaned, then he sniffed, and at last a great sob came up from inside him and two large tears rolled down his cheeks, splashed onto his hands, and from there bounced onto the floor in drops of gold.

Chapter Three

The Price

*T*he King, in his misery, hadn't noticed that he was not alone.

In through the french windows, open on the garden, had come a friend of his – a very dear friend, though not a human one. (Kings have some problems with human friends. It's hard for them to be sure that people like them for themselves, and not just so they can go around saying they're friends with a king.)

This friend, being a dog, cared absolutely nothing for anyone's opinion except his master's. His name was Stray, which explains how the King got him – he'd just wandered into the palace grounds one day when he was a forlorn lost puppy, the head gardener had brought him to the King and the King had given him to Delia. But dogs make their own arrangements as to whom they belong to. Stray belonged to Midas.

Stray sensed, the moment he came in, that all was not well. He thought the King's bad mood might be due to something *he* had done, such as burying a certain bone in a certain rose-bed. So he slunk under the table, hoping for better times.

But then he heard strange noises – a sigh, a groan, a sob. Such sounds are very upsetting to a dog. Stray poked his nose out from under the golden cloth. He saw a familiar, and dear, hand hanging limply from the arm of the chair, and, as much as to say, "Cheer up, boss, how's about a walk, eh?" he nuzzled his nose into the palm of it.

That was the last thing Stray knew.

Even as the King felt the gentle touch of Stray's tongue against his hand, the warmth went out of it. It became cold and hard. Midas gave a cry of horror, and snatched his hand away. But too late.

Beside his chair stood Stray, not the dog he knew, friendly, full of life, sensitive to the King's every mood, but a lifeless golden statue.

The King fell to his knees on the floor and embraced this – object. It felt repulsive to his touch. His eyes screwed up to shut out the hateful sight. Shame and regret welled up in his heart and sorrow almost choked him.

"Oh, blind, greed-crazed fool that I am," he cried. "What have I done?"

But the pictures behind his tight-shut eyes were relentless. The rose, lifeless and scentless; the deathly, empty trees; the little bird with its sightless eyes; and now this – his faithful friend. He imagined them warm and living, and saw them now, cold and dead.

And he got up from his knees and ran to the open windows that led to the garden, to the place where the magician had told him to go to find him again.

But as he reached them, a great flash of lightning lit up the room. There was a roar of thunder, and the rain began pouring down in torrential streams so heavy he could see nothing but water. As it fell on his hands, it bounced onto the sodden ground in shining drops, and suddenly a zigzag of lightning struck hissing and flashing at the metal, like a giant's pitchfork.

Be sure it's not raining! The magician's mocking last words sounded again in Midas' ears.

Midas made one heroic effort to go out. He was drenched to the skin in two seconds. The lightning struck at his feet again, making him jump back into the dining-room – he couldn't stop himself. He slammed the windows behind him, locked them, and leant against them, trembling with fright.

There was a strange silence. He raised his eyes. The french windows, glass and all, had turned to gold. The storm, the night, the garden, were closed off from his sight. When he tried tentatively to open them, he found they had fused into a solid gold wall. Of course, there were other ways out, but . . .

"I shall wait until tomorrow," he muttered.

He went slowly upstairs to his bedroom, his head down, dragging his feet, and not even noticing how his magic made the gold shoot along the banisters. He was trying to keep from weeping because Stray was not trotting up after him, and then he thought of something even worse.

Delia!

Of course there was no question of going to her room as he always did, every night, to chat to her and tuck her into bed. Though he had never, ever needed her more . . . But the danger! No, he mustn't, anything could happen!

What, then, am I never to see her again –? But he couldn't face that terrible thought.

"I'll try to sleep," he told himself. "Tomorrow the weather will be better. I'll go to the rose-garden and say –" For one appalling second he thought he'd forgotten the magic words, but then they came back to him: "'Red rose, bloom again'. He'll come, that fiend – no, no, not fair, mustn't blame him, he gave me a chance to think and I didn't, I didn't! Oh, was there ever a man so stupid! – Anyway, he'll return, and heaven alone knows what he'll want as a fee this time, but whatever it is he shall have it, even if it's half my kingdom or ten years of my life, just so I can be rid of this ghastly curse I've brought down on my idiotic old head!"

Biffpot was waiting in the King's dressing-room. The servants' quarters were alive with the most terrible rumours. Several of the staff had packed up and left. But Biffpot was devoted to the King, and determined that he would be the last to desert his employer, who had always been very good to him.

"Are you retiring early, Sire?" he asked, trying to keep his voice quite normal.

"Yes, Biffpot," said the King, and then, as the man made a step towards him, he suddenly shouted:

"Keep back, man, don't come near me!"

Biffpot started back. The King was very agitated and kept his hands behind him. They stared at each other.

"Will you – disrobe yourself, Sire?" asked Biffpot at last.

The King was breathing heavily, and frowning.

"No. I must have help with – my clothes," he said at last in a strangled voice. "There must be – some answer – to my immediate problems. Ah . . . Biffpot, the gauntlets!"

"Sire?"

"The cloth-of-gold gauntlet gloves that I wore at my coronation! They are gold already, it may be that . . . Yes, it's worth a try! Fetch them, Biffpot, they are in the Royal Robing Room. You have the keys . . . Be quick, there's a good fellow!"

Biffpot was back in a few minutes with a magnificent pair of high-cuffed gloves, very thick and heavy, woven of pure gold thread and richly embroidered.

"Good. Put them there, on the chair."

The man obeyed. The King snatched up one glove. Biffpot, watching closely, thought he saw the embroidery lose its colour as the King pulled the gauntlet on. The same thing happened with the other glove. Then the King did a curious thing – he touched the chair, the wall, the door-handle with his gloved fingers, cautiously, as if they might be red hot. He breathed a deep sigh of relief.

"These might make all the difference . . . But still, I cannot take the slightest risk. Biffpot, turn down the bedclothes. I shall sleep as I am – if I can sleep at all."

"Sleep *in your clothes*, Sire!"

"It doesn't matter, Biffpot."

Biffpot uneasily turned back the bedclothes and the King climbed heavily into bed. He was shivering and sweating. Biffpot, very concerned, spread two more blankets. The King was ashy pale.

"Are you unwell, Sire?"

"I think I may have caught a chill. I got wet in the storm."

"Storm, Sire? When was that?"

Midas raised his head from the pillow. "Just now."

"It's a fine evening, Sire. No rain for a week."

The King stared at him. "A magic storm then," he whispered. "I see it is all to be made as hard for me as possible . . . Quite right. Quite right!" His voice shook.

"Sire?"

"Never mind, Biffpot. Go to the Princess and tell her — tell her I have a cold and can't come to her this evening. Give her . . ." he cleared his throat and passed a hand across his eyes. "Give her my love, will you, and say — I will see her tomorrow after school. By then, everything will be . . . I have the best hope that . . ." He kept the gauntlet pressed to his eyes and Biffpot saw that he couldn't say any more.

"Goodnight, Sire," he said quietly, and withdrew from the room, a deeply troubled man.

Princess Delia was sitting up in bed drinking cocoa, waiting for her father and reflecting on the day.

It had been a good one. She had got up earlier than usual because the weather was so perfect, and the birdsong so loud. Still in her nightdress, she had run to feed and talk to her birds in the aviary in her playroom. She had seven different kinds, but her favourite was a plain grey parrot with a red spot on his tail. He could say lots of things, but his favourite thing to say was, "I am a prince in disguise!" Delia had taught him that and it kept all her friends guessing.

Then she had run downstairs and out into the conservatory to have her bath. This really was rather special; the King had had it made for her as a special surprise last birthday, and the thrill of it had not yet worn off.

The conservatory was huge, and very warm,

and filled with tropical plants. She had to push through them to get to her bath. It was sunk into the floor, and made like a woodland pool large enough to swim in. It was lined with natural stone, and real moss. The water – just hot enough, and smelling of exotic flowers – flowed down from a hidden source above. There were real birds flying about, and it was just like being in a jungle.

When she'd played and swum as much as she wanted to, she pressed a certain rock on the edge of the pool. Her personal maid appeared around a yucca plant with a big, warm, fluffy towel. She would wrap herself up in this and dash back upstairs to dress.

She had a lot of clothes to choose from, apart from her special ones for wearing on state occasions. But for school she wore what her friends wore, only maybe a little bit nicer. The school uniform was a plain brown tunic with a white blouse, buttoned with pearl buttons. Nobody knew that the buttons on Delia's blouse were real pearl or that the tunic was as light as a cobweb and fashioned out of the underfur of a musk-ox. And she never told them.

In summer she had her breakfast on a terrace overlooking the roses. It was daintily prepared and brought to her on a silver tray – always more or less the same: passionfruit or mango juice, a cereal made of mixed grains and dried fruit, and one peacock egg perfectly boiled, with

her slice of buttered wheat-toast cut into fingers for dipping. The egg was so big she only ate the yolk.

She was driven to school in a pony-trap because it was too far to walk. She was allowed to drive it herself, though a groom always went with her to look after her. He had been a seafaring man, and had a fund of stories that never seemed to run out.

School was a mixed pleasure, usually, but today had been a good day there, too. Her homework was all done and all right, for once. Her best friend, with whom she had had a silly quarrel, came to make it up. She auditioned for the end-of-year play and got – not the best part, but the second best, which was more than she'd hoped for. She was very excited about this, and was longing to tell her father.

After school the pony-trap and the groom had been waiting to take her to a friend's house for tea. This had been arranged in advance (princesses can't do very much on the spur of the moment, unfortunately.) There was a certain amount of bowing and curtseying and far too rich a tea for Delia's taste, but that always happened – she had had to get used to it, all her friends' parents did it. But this time at least she and her friend were able to get away to the playroom afterwards and have fun on their own without any fuss. She got home rather late, and had hurried straight to her own quarters to do her homework before bedtime. (She went to bed very early in term-time. The lives of princesses are apt to be highly regulated.)

All this explains why she had not seen her father all day.

Now she was all ready for sleep; this was his time to come – he never failed to come to tuck her in and exchange news about their days. So when the gentle knock came on the door, she called happily:

"Come in, Daddy!"

When Biffpot appeared, her face fell. "Oh, hallo, Biffpot. Where's the King?" she asked.

"He is unwell, Your Highness," Biffpot said with the customary bow. "He sends Your Highness his love and apologies."

Delia sat straight up in bed, her face full of anxiety.

"What's wrong with him?"

Biffpot coughed and lowered his eyes. He was not a good liar.

"A slight cold, Your Highness, nothing worse."

"Oh. Well. Thank you. Goodnight."

Biffpot, who was of the old school of royal retainers, backed out of the room, closing the door softly. The Princess thought for a moment, put down her mug, and pressed the bell for her maid.

Nobody came.

This was very strange. Her father had always come. The maid had always come . . . She had been with her earlier to help her get ready for bed. She'd seemed oddly nervous . . .

Delia now noticed an oddness about the palace. She couldn't put her finger on it. It just seemed quieter than usual, as if it contained fewer people.

It was not usually her job to put the light out, but tonight she had to, and lay down to sleep. But she couldn't. She kept thinking of her father with his cold. These were the times he must specially miss having a queen. *She* would have seen that he had enough bedclothes and made sure someone brought him a honey-and-lemon drink.

She wondered if he had a hot-water bottle. He had once told her men didn't need them, but she thought this was ridiculous. Nobody can fall asleep with cold feet! She snuggled her feet against her own hot-water bottle, and suddenly she had an idea.

She would take him *hers*. She would tiptoe into his room and slip it into his bed.

So she got up, put on her dressing-gown and slippers, and crept quietly through the darkened palace to the King's bedroom.

"How quiet it is," she thought as she slipped along the wide, carpetted corridors. "Where is everybody tonight?"

The King lay in his bed, on his back, snoring slightly, only his head and hands outside the covers. She stood with the hot-water bottle in her hand, looking down at him. He was very pale and had a lost, sad look. She felt her love for him very strongly suddenly, like a pain, and bent down to give him a feather-light kiss that wouldn't wake him.

That's when she noticed the gauntlets.

"Why ever is he wearing those huge gloves?" she thought. "He'll be so uncomfortable!"

And she gently eased the first onc off, and then began to tuck his hand under the covers so it wouldn't get cold.

Chapter Four

The Quest Begins

When the King woke up next morning, his nose was blocked up solid. He reached his hand under his pillow to feel for a handkerchief. At once he felt as if his head was resting on a huge, icy stone.

His eyes flew open with a sudden awful feeling of foreboding.

The first thing he saw was his right hand – his treacherous, enchanted hand, ungloved and deadly, in front of his face. And then, as if it would say, *There! See my masterpiece!* it moved aside by itself, and the blood rushed from the King's face to sustain a heart that had all but stopped beating.

Delia stood bent over him in her long night-gown. Her curls, which had been gold to begin with, fell over her shoulders. In her hand was a golden hot-water bottle.

Everything about her – from her eyelashes to the fur on her bedroom slippers – was modelled in gold more perfectly than any master sculptor could have made it. On her face was a look of tender concern, frozen now into deathly stillness.

The King could only stare and stare, numb with the shock of it. Then he started up. He stripped the other gauntlet from his hand, and began frantically stroking her hair and rubbing her little hands as if he could bring life back into them.

But she was stiff and cold.

He didn't rail or weep or accuse himself, as he had over his dog. It was too bad for that. His greed had murdered his child. Here she was before him – final proof of his folly.

Now he did something from habit too strong to be broken. He reached for the locket that held his dead queen's hair. He had done this for years, whenever he needed comfort and courage. He started as his fingers touched it.

"Not that too!" he cried brokenly.

He lifted it from his neck, opened it – gold as it had always been – and found that by some wonder, the lock of hair behind the glass was still real.

He stared at it for a long time. What power had protected it against his curse? Could it be love – or his queen, reaching out to him somehow from beyond the grave? The sight of the lock he had touched so many times gave him a morsel of hope. A hope against hope that somehow Delia still lived.

He clicked the locket shut and hung it round his neck, the one real, true thing that was left to him. A little courage came to him.

He thought of the magic storm, his retreat last night. He knew that he faced a great ordeal and that however bad it was, he must do his best, and better than his best. If he couldn't find a remedy his life was as good as over.

He got up, turning all the bedclothes into gold without even noticing. In his dressing-room was a beautiful screen. He dragged it – monstrously heavy as it suddenly was – to the bedside and set its folds around his golden daughter. Then he rang the bell – brass before he touched it, pure gold afterwards.

After a long time there was a timid knock.

"Is that you, Biffpot?"

"Y-y-yes, Sire," said a shaky voice.

"Come in."

Biffpot's face, white with fear, came round the door.

"What's the matter with you, man?" asked the King.

Biffpot hardly knew how to answer. The palace below and all around them was empty. Not another servant had dared to stay after it was discovered that the Princess had disappeared – nobody could face the King with such news.

"Her Royal Highness, Your Majesty, she's –"

"Silence on that subject, Biffpot," said the King quietly.

Biffpot bowed obediently, but his eyes were taking in the room, the golden objects the King had touched, the mysterious screen by the bed, the gauntlets on the floor ... The gauntlets! Biffpot's eyes flew to the King's hands. They were uncovered and slightly raised, the fingers twitching as if they had life of their own. He gasped and took a step backward instinctively.

"Yes, Biffpot. You do well to keep away from these hands," said the King, holding them up in front of his face and staring at them with loathing. "I fear I may not be in control of them for much longer. You see before you a desperate man ... I must go. I must go."

"Where are you going, Sire?"

"Into the garden. After that ... Heaven knows ... I don't. Meanwhile, my dear old fellow ... allow me to call you that, you are far more like a friend to me than a valet, and I suspect that you alone have not deserted me as I deserve ... I want you to do for me what may be a last service. Do you see that screen?"

"I see it, Sire."

"Behind that screen is the greatest treasure in my kingdom. You are the only person I can trust to guard it with your life until I come back. Will you do that for me?"

"Yes, Sire."

"Thank you," said the King simply. "I hope I won't be away too long."

"Don't you need your – gloves, Sire?"

The King paused at the door. "They are useless to me now," he said strangely. "Everything is useless except courage. Of which I have never had much. Goodbye, my friend."

The King left the palace by the main doors. As soon as he stepped outside, the magic storm began again, just as it had before. But now the King had no time to be afraid. He rushed out like a madman, dodging the flashes of lightning that stabbed down at him, and ran to the rose garden.

The elements seemed to burst themselves in an effort to stop him. When he tried to call out "Red rose, bloom again!" his voice was drowned by the thunder. The louder he shouted the words, the more the noise of the storm seemed to mock him – the lightning formed a ring of fire around him, the rain dashed into his mouth, the thunder half deafened him, the wind carried his words away.

At last he stopped trying to make himself heard, and stood still. "I will wait," he said inside his head. "I will stand here all day if I must! Even a magic storm can't last for ever.""

The thunder rolled as if to say, "Oh yes, it can!" But the King was thinking of Delia and didn't hear.

"I'll do anything to undo what I've done," he vowed to himself. "I'll live in a hermit's cave in rags, and eat nuts and berries. I hope with all my heart I never see gold again for the rest of my life. *She* is all that matters."

And he meant every word.

Thoughts are magic, too, though the King didn't know it. Abruptly, he saw the sun dazzling through the golden leaves and making diamonds on the wet grass. Across the black clouds, grumbling away into the distance, stretched a rainbow full of every colour but gold.

The King sighed heavily, cleared his throat and said loudly:

"Red rose, bloom again!"

At first, nothing seemed to happen. The King's battered heart sank. But then suddenly, there was the Midas rose, just as it had been the day before, glowing with all its reds, all by itself in the air – floating quietly in front of the King, at the height of his waist.

He felt his right hand move towards the rose without his order, and he couldn't stop it. It was the most awful feeling. The rose moved out of reach.

The old man's voice out of nowhere said, "None of that! You have lots of roses of your own to turn into gold. I prefer mine as it is."

"So do I!" said the King.

The old magician appeared all at once, in a flash of green light. The rose was still pinned to his leather waistcoat.

"Say it," he said sharply.

The King understood what he had to do.

"I hate gold," he said, slowly and clearly. "I

have been worse than a fool. I've destroyed all
that I love best. I'm in despair. Help me, I beg
of you. Take away this curse."

The magician seemed to be thinking of something else. He stroked his long white beard and
drew out of it a long black cigar.

"Oh, please, listen to me!" begged the King.
"Hm?"

The little man put the cigar into his mouth.
It was already alight, but instead of having a
red glow at the end, it had a green one. And
when it was puffed, the smoke that came out of
Nandan's mouth was green too.

"Hate gold, eh?" he said, puffing. "Too bad.
Have to live with it for the rest of your life."

"Don't! Oh, don't say that!" cried the King
in anguish. "Don't tell me you won't take the
spell off!"

"No 'won't' about it," replied Nandan, blowing a green smoke-ring. "Can't. I don't know
how."

The King felt as if he'd been hit in the stomach.
"But if you can't, who can?" he gasped out.

"Hard to say," said the magician. He flicked
away a piece of ash. As it landed on the ground,
it turned into a little green bird, which took off
suddenly from the grass and flew away singing.

The King didn't notice. "You *must* help me!"
he pleaded desperately. "I'll give you anything
you ask!"

The magician looked at him for the first time,
and his eyes, which looked surprisingly young

in such a wrinkled old face, twinkled more than ever. Midas suddenly knew what they reminded him of – a mask with eyes looking through it.

"*Anything?*" Nandan asked sharply.

"Anything in my power," replied Midas.

"Hm," said the little man.

He stuck the cigar between his teeth and walked up and down with his hands behind his back. His beard was so long that he often had to kick it out of his way. Each time a piece of ash fell from the cigar, it turned into a little green bird.

"Do you give your word? Anything I ask?"

"Yes, yes!" cried the King. "Only please hurry!"

"You should never use that word to a man of magic," said Nandan. "It is not polite." At this moment he tripped over his beard and fell flat on his face, but as he was falling he worked a spell that made the ground in front of him turn into a feather mattress.

"Now," he continued, making himself comfortable on it. "I am a very lonely magician. I've been lonely for hundreds of years, so I can wait a few more. Just until that beautiful daughter of yours is old enough to get married."

The King gasped.

"You don't mean you want *her* as a reward for –"

"Seven years from now," Nandan said, "or eight at the most, I shall come and marry

her. Unless, of course," he added carelessly, blowing another series of green smoke-rings at the sky, "you'd rather keep her for ever – as she is."

The King was silent.

I originally mentioned that the King had one fault. You may have noticed at least one other – the tendency to lose his temper. Now I have to reveal a third.

Since he had lost his queen, the thought of one day losing Delia too – though differently – had set up an unnatural rebellion in his heart. He dreaded the loneliness he would feel when what he thought of as "some young whippersnapper" came to carry her off.

If anyone had asked him, "What, you mean she's to be an old maid, just to give you company in your old age?" he would have been shocked. No, no, he was not so selfish! But he would not part with her to just *any* young whippersnapper. It was no more than a father's duty to be rigorously selective.

So he had let it be known that he would never give her hand in marriage, unless it should be to a royal prince who could grow a better rose than the King.

This sounded quite reasonable – no prince ever married a princess unless he could prove he had *something* special going for him. But in fact, it actually meant that Delia would never marry at all, because the King was one of the best – if not the *very* best rose grower in the world. Princes,

I might add, are not known as good gardeners, in fact most of them wouldn't know a trowel from a rhododendron.

But now here was a difficulty Midas had not foreseen. Either he had to promise that when Delia was eighteen she should marry this little old magician, or keep her for ever as a golden statue.

He thought and thought, while the little man lay in front of him on his mattress, smoking and playing with his long beard. At last the King gave a deep sigh and said:

"Very well. If you can tell me how to bring Delia back to life, and take the magic off my hands, you have my permission to marry her. *But only if she wants to.*"

"That," said the magician, leaping nimbly to his feet, "goes without saying." With a wave of his hand he turned the mattress into a box-hedge shaped like a wedding cake.

"This means she is alive?" said the King eagerly.

"She is, and she isn't," said Nandan. "She isn't at this moment, and nor will she ever be again unless we can bring off one of the most difficult tricks in the book – the reversal of a permanent spell. I admit it's beyond *my* powers, but there are those more learned in the magic arts than myself, who ... Alas, not all of them are as benign as I ... in fact, some of the cleverest are really very wicked indeed ... We must hope you don't have to resort to one of that kind, or the price I have requested will seem as nothing."

The King swallowed. The magician produced a red leather thinking-cap out of the air and put it on.

"Got to get your hands right – that's the first priority," he said. "The only possible hope for that is Old Gollop."

"Old who?"

"Old Gollop is the Father of the River Cijam."

"I've never heard of such a river. It can't be in my kingdom."

"Ah, but it is. When it can be found at all. Among us it's known as Cijam, which is 'magic' backwards, because it can de-spell all kinds of things."

"What do you mean, 'when it can be found at all'? Isn't it in a fixed place?"

"Yes . . . no . . . Oh really, it's very hard to explain to one outside the magic fraternity. You have to be *shown*, I mean *led* – that is, someone has to –"

Suddenly he stopped, and stood with one hand to his ear as if trying to catch some faint but vitally important call.

"Too bad!" he said in his cracked voice. "Have to go. Sorry."

With that, he started to melt, like butter on a hot plate, very quickly into the ground. Before the King could grasp what was happening, he had melted almost right away.

"Stop! Come back! Bread loze, loom aben, I

mean – Led hose, broom amen – I mean, DON'T LEAVE ME!" gibbered the King. "You must tell me how to find Old Whatsisname!"

Out of the blob that was all that was left of the magician, a slurry voice, like syrup pouring, said: "The ash-birds know!" Then the blob sank into the ground and was gone.

Chapter Five

Old Gollop

*I*f the King had had a beard, he would have
pulled it right off with frustration. But after
a while, he stopped dancing up and down with
rage, and started to think.

The ash-birds know!

What could the ash-birds be?

Then he remembered. Of course! The little
green birds that magically flew away whenever
a bit of ash fell off Nandan's black cigar!

But how could he find one?

He felt so hopeless about it that he sat down
in the grass and put his head in his hands. After
a moment, he began to cough.

At first he thought this was just part of the awful
cold he had (he was still soaking wet from the
rain.) But it wasn't that kind of cough. It was a
tickle in his throat. And suddenly he noticed that a
thin curl of smoke was floating up from the grass.

Green smoke.

He peered down, and there, sure enough, was the butt-end of the black cigar, still alight, with a little piece of green ash on the end!

"Saved!" he all but shouted. "Now all I have to do is pick it up, and —"

The treacherous right hand was actually reaching towards the cigar, when Midas, unable to stop it, rolled violently away, dragging the hand after him.

"Not this time, you don't," he growled at his own hand, which drooped from his wrist as if disappointed that its plot had been foiled.

Holding his right hand in his left, behind his back, he rolled over onto his knees and, very uncomfortably because of his round stomach, put his face into the grass. With great difficulty he managed to get the cigar-butt between his lips.

He lifted his head cautiously so as not to disturb the ash, and puffed and puffed till there was hardly anything left of the cigar at all. Midas was not a smoker, and the smoke from this cigar was ferociously strong. It stung his nostrils, his eyes, and worst of all, his throat, but he dared not let himself cough.

Just when his lips were going to get burnt if he puffed once more, the piece of ash fell off at last.

Up from the grass flew the little green ash-bird. Midas dropped the cigar and scrambled to his feet. Over the box-hedge and away across the palace garden went the tiny bird, with the King in hot and breathless pursuit.

It was lucky that the ash-bird didn't fly through the town. People would have thought it very strange to see their King, puffing and panting, with his face turned up to keep his small guide in sight, running through the streets of the capital.

Instead, the bird led him across fields and meadows, through gates and over stiles, along country lanes and under the branches of trees. The King had no idea where they were going because he was looking up all the time, which is how it happened that he suddenly found himself face down in a foot of ice-cold water.

By the time he had picked himself up, soaking wet once more from head to foot, the ash-bird was nowhere in sight.

He looked around in all directions.

He was standing up to his calves in a quiet little river that ran between two meadows. On his right it disappeared into a clump of trees. On his left, it twisted out of sight among some rocks that were the beginning of a range of hills. Except for a cow, peacefully chewing the cud near him, there wasn't a living thing in sight.

"What can I do *now*?" the King asked himself. "My ash-bird has gone, and I've no idea where I am."

He was so wet! Surely the first thing to do was to wring out his clothes. He took off his shirt first and began wringing the sleeves. When he'd got as much river-water out of it as possible, he laid it on the bank in the sun, before removing his trousers and his vest for the same treatment.

It was only when he took his shoes off to empty the water out of them that he stopped dead.

He stared at the wet shoe in his hands. Then his eyes snapped to the clothes laid out to dry. The shoe was made of leather and the clothes were made of cloth. *Still.*

The King felt as if a black monster that had been crouching on his back had suddenly flown away. He leapt to his bare feet and began capering about in his underpants, filled with joy and relief.

"Hooray!" he shouted, like a schoolboy again. "It's the River Cijam! I've found it! I'm saved! Delia's saved! We're all saved! Hooray!"

The cow looked at him in surprise.

"Dear cow!" cried the King, lost to all sense of decorum. "I'm all right again. Look! I can stroke you!" And he did.

And she turned into solid gold.

The black monster, having had a little flap around, settled itself back upon poor Midas, who almost collapsed with disappointment.

But he pulled himself together again quickly.

He had to understand this. He rushed back to the river and dabbled his fingers in the water. It stayed water. He picked up some pebbles from the bed of the stream. He pulled a swaying weed that grew up from the bottom. They stayed as they were.

He was baffled. He wiped his wet hand on the grass to dry it, and then he noticed something. The first wipe changed nothing. But with the second wipe, a few leaf-edges and blades of grass became gold. His hand was dry now. He laid it on the bank and lifted it. There was the outline of his hand in gold, made up of grass-blades and tiny leaves and flowers.

"Ah! So that's it!"

It was the River Cijam all right, and its waters were powerful enough to fight the magic. His wet clothes were resistant. The water itself could not be affected, and while his hands were wet, all was safe from their enchantment. But as soon as they were dry . . .

"But Nandan said the river could de-spell me," he thought. "Here, it clearly can't . . . I still have my cursed magic touch! I shall have to find Old Gollop. He's the Father of the River. So I must follow it into the hills until I find its source."

He sat down, with unusual patience, to wait until his clothes were more or less dry. Then, dipping his hands often to keep them wet, he dressed himself and put on his shoes.

He left the golden cow standing in the field and began to walk along by the river. Soon the path grew steeper and steeper until he was turning rocks and trees and bushes into gold by using them to pull himself upward.

By this time the river no longer flowed along quietly, but splashed past him over waterfalls. He noticed that as the way got steeper, the river was getting smaller, narrower and shallower.

At last he was very high up in the hills. The river here was no more than a trickle, hurrying down over the stones in a series of waterfalls. He was getting very tired by now, but he'd forgotten his hunger until he saw some berries on a briar.

"Ah! Blackberries! Careful, now . . ."

It was hard to bite them off and he got his face badly scratched, but they tasted wonderful – wonderful! Even the few he managed to eat helped allay his hunger pangs. He wondered if they might be magic, too, so near to this extraordinary river.

He rounded a bend in the path, and all at once, up ahead of him, he saw it! A great rock in the shape of a huge head – an old man's head. Out of its mouth poured the beginnings of the river.

"That's him!" the King realised at once, and panted up the last few yards, certain in his heart that the end of his quest was in sight.

But just as he reached the rock, a strange thing happened.

The water stopped flowing. The last trickle ran out of the gaping mouth, down the hillside – and no more followed.

"Excuse me," said the King. "Are you by any chance Old Gollop?"

"I am," replied the rock in a rumbling, grinding voice.

Breathlessly the King explained his plight, and his errand.

"Ah! If you'd only come ten minutes ago," grated Old Gollop, "I could have helped you. You see, to take the spell off for good, you would have to wash your hands in the river where it first comes out of my mouth. That is where the anti-spelling power of the water is strongest. But I'm sorry to say my throat has been blocked up by that old witch, Wuzzleflump, and unless something is done, the River Cijam will just . . ." he wheezed for a moment. "Dry – up," he said at last, ominously.

He gave a heavy sigh, like the wind round an old stone house.

"I'm losing my voice, too," he said indistinctly.

"But that's appalling!" cried the King. "How can we clear your throat?"

"There's only one thing that would do it," wheezed Old Gollop gloomily. "And you know what that is."

"No I don't!"

"A flandy-bake, naturally."

"A what?"

The old rock sighed again, pityingly this time. "You are obviously a very ill-educated person," he said sorrowfully. "Flandy-bakes are highly effective, and extremely tasty, anti-witchidants." Midas looked perfectly blank. "Anti – *witch* – Oh, never mind! Can you get me one, that's the question?"

"I could try," said the King eagerly. "If I only knew what I was looking for."

There was a deep, grinding, growling sound

from deep in the rock as Old Gollop cleared his throat a little.

"Magic – fruits –" he ground out. "Grow – trees – witch – stole – feed – mumbo—"

Midas was beginning to panic. Gollop's voice was almost inaudible now, and he seemed to be talking nonsense.

"Where is the witch?" he shouted into a crevice he took to be Gollop's ear.

"Not – deaf –" whispered the rock.

"Sorry! Sorry! But please – try to tell me!"

Gollop gave a cough that sounded like grind-stones rubbing together, and screeched out with the very last of his voice: "Behind – seventh – fall – mind – mumbo!"

And that incomprehensible word was the last Midas could get out of him. The King said a respectful goodbye and started scrambling down the hillside again.

He might be stupid about some things, but Midas was quite quick on the uptake about others. "Behind seventh fall" made instant sense to him. The trouble was, as there was no more water to make waterfalls, it was difficult to count them; but it was all right, because when he got to the seventh he saw that, behind where the water would have been, if there had been any, was a little wooden door.

It was streaked with wet green mosses, and a big ugly fungus grew out of it in three layers. The handle and hinges were old and thick with rust, and there was a notice under a bellrope that said:

RING WRONG
SING SONG
BEWARE OF THE MUMBO!

"Now then," thought the King. "I must be careful." Though he had never personally encountered a witch, he knew they were not to be fooled around with. According to his information, Riddling Witches were the most dangerous kind.

"'Ring wrong'," mused the King. "Well. How would one ring if one were ringing *right*? One would *pull* a bellrope, of course. So as I've been told to ring *wrong*, I'll try pushing it."

The rope, when pushed upwards, gave a quick wiggle and disappeared into its hole above the door like a golden snake (for of course, it was gold by then).

Just as the King was wondering what sort of song to sing when the witch came to answer the door, it creaked open by itself, and the King saw a long, dark passage ahead of him, leading straight into the heart of the hill. It smelt of damp and rot, and had long stalactites hanging from the roof like greenish swords waiting to fall.

The King needed to sing, to keep up his courage. He made up a song on the spot that fitted the occasion:

"What can a Mumbo be?
It is unknown to me!

I hope that if I meet – ONE! –
I'll see it before it sees me!"

He kept his voice steady with an effort, and stepped forward into the dripping tunnel. No sooner was he inside the door than it creaked shut behind him, leaving him in total darkness.

Chapter Six

The Witch's Cave

*M*idas had to feel his way along the mossy-wet stone wall, every now and then bumping his face on a stalactite. He had never thought of himself as a brave man, and he was very much afraid now, but there was no question in his mind of not going on. He'd known it wouldn't be easy – he didn't *deserve* it to be easy.

But in his mind were some awesome pictures. One was of a witch's lair, complete with witch, her warty nose curving to her chin, straggly hair under a pointed black hat, stirring a cauldron of poison and stroking a black cat. Her stroking hand was long and knobbly, and had *green nails*.

The other was of a strange monster like a vast black balloon with a terrifying face. This was his notion of a mumbo, a creature he had never even heard of.

He shivered, and began his song again:

"What can a mumbo –"

"Great song," said a voice beside him.

Midas nearly jumped out of his skin, and found himself flattened against the cold wall, trembling all over.

"Are you – harrumph! – Witch Wuzzleflump?" he croaked.

Whoever the voice belonged to burst into a noisy laugh.

"Of course I'm not!" it said. "I'm the mumbo you were singing about, and I'm going to eat you. Pity in a way. Liked the song."

"I could – make up another verse about you – if you like," said the King quickly, trying to control his breathing.

There was a pause.

"Would there be long words in it?"

"Oh yes, I know lots of long words!" said the King hastily.

Another thoughtful pause, and then the voice said, "No. Sorry. Can't wait. I'm starving."

Midas suddenly remembered, in his extremity, that Gollop had said something about the witch taking the flandy-bakes to feed her mumbo. So he choked out through his terror: "Haven't you eaten any flandy-bakes lately?"

Midas felt the Thing shuffle closer. He could smell its breath now. It had a sinister smoky smell.

"Who told you about those?" it hissed.

"All the best mumbos feed on them," said the King, rather cleverly.

There was a long pause, and then the Mumbo said craftily, "Perhaps I won't eat you just yet. I'll have a competition with you first."

"A – a what did you say?" asked the King in bewilderment.

"You're not deaf, are you?" the Mumbo asked rudely. Its voice was odd, not like a monster's, more like the voice of a cheeky little boy. Suddenly it was shouting in the King's ear: "A COMPETITION, I said! You know what a COMPETITION is, I suppose?"

"I think so," said the King, banging his ear, which nearly *was* deaf by now.

"It's a thing – where you both – try to do something – better than the other," said the Mumbo very slowly, as if the King were a half-wit. "Got that? With ours, whoever wins gets to eat the one who loses."

"No," said the King bravely. "If I win, you must take me to see Witch Wuzzleflump."

The mumbo burst into sniggers. "Why not? You can't possibly beat me. The COMPETITION is to see who can throw the furthest."

"But there's no light to see by," objected the King, "so how can we know who's won?"

"*I* can see in the dark," said the mumbo smugly.

"Well, I can't," said the King, "so you can't call it a fair COMPETITION." He roared the word, like the mumbo. Heaven knows how he dared.

"All right, all right, no need to shout," it said. It had moved further away and now seemed to be round a corner. "I'll give you some light since you're so fussy."

There was a little click. All along the roof, and in holes in the walls, glow-worms lit up.

The King instantly turned his eyes to the place where the mumbo's voice had come from.

"I'm behind you," it said. "Don't look round. If you see me, I'll eat you *on the spot*."

The King swallowed hard and faced straight ahead, down the tunnel.

"Do you see that big pointed thing up ahead, hanging from the roof?"

"The stalactite, you mean?"

"Is *that* what it's called? Stal-ac-tite." It rolled the syllables round its mouth. "Hm! I like it. I love long words. Well, anyway, the one that comes nearest to hitting it, wins."

The King had been a cricket-player in his youth. He thought he might do quite well at this.

"What shall we throw?"

The mumbo, behind him, sniggered again.

"Feathers."

"You can't throw feathers," protested the King. "No matter how hard you throw one, it just floats to the ground."

"Of course if you'd rather not play, you could be eaten instead."

"I'll play," said the King.

"Good," said the Mumbo. "Reach your hand back, and I'll give you your feather."

The King obeyed. As soon as he felt the feather in his hand he closed his fingers round it and said, "You go first."

"No, you," said the mumbo.

"All the best mumbos go first," said the King.

"Oh. Yes. Forgot that. All right then," it said. "But of course, as I'm standing behind you, it wouldn't be *fair* if I threw just what you're throwing. You'd be sure to win. So my feather has a dart stuck to it."

It gave another snort of laughter, and a feathered dart flew past the King's ear.

But the Mumbo wasn't really trying very hard, because it didn't think for a minute that the King's plain feather could possibly beat it. The dart missed the stalactite by several inches.

The King carefully aimed his solid gold feather, and threw it. It whizzed through the air and struck the stalactite squarely, making a satisfying ping.

"I win," said the King, trying not to sound too pleased about it.

There was an ominous silence from behind him. Then the mumbo said sulkily, "You did something tricky."

"A trick for a trick," said Midas. "So now will you take me to see the witch?"

"I couldn't do that," said the Mumbo. "She wouldn't like it."

"But you promised!"

"Everyone knows mumbos don't have to keep

promises," said the mumbo triumphantly – and Midas felt its smoky breath on his neck. "Well, goodbye. I'm going to eat you now."

But the King still had a trick up his sleeve – well, just outside it. He swung round with his fist.

He felt his hand hit something, and at that moment all the glow-worms went off. The mumbo must have knocked the switch as it was turning into gold. The King couldn't see what it looked like, and he wasn't much bothered. He left the golden mumbo behind and felt his way further along the passage.

Soon he saw a gleam of light, and when he reached it he saw it was a notice, lit by glow-worms, which said: WITCH WAY

"Is that the name of the witch's home, or is it a question?" mused the King. On either side of the sign, the tunnel divided. Both ways looked dark and uninviting, and the King felt sure he would run into more dangers if he took the wrong one – possibly fall into a pot-hole or something.

As he dithered, he felt something soft brush against his legs. He looked down, and by the faint light of the glow-worms he saw a black cat. It turned its glowing green eyes on him for a moment, and then slipped away – down the left-hand tunnel.

The King followed it into total darkness. But it didn't stay dark for long.

Twenty yards further on, the passage turned a corner, and almost at once widened out into quite a large cave. It was brightly lit by lanterns, and as the King looked around he saw shelves of dusty bottles full of odd-coloured powders and liquids; some enormous books with pages yellowed by age; bunches of leaves and herbs hanging from the ceiling, and a big besom against the wall. A snow-white owl sat in the chimney-corner, silently staring at him. A great fire burned in the fireplace under a black cauldron, and bent over the cauldron, stirring its contents and mumbling to herself, was the witch.

So far it was just what the King had pictured. But when the witch turned round, he got a surprise.

She wasn't an ugly old hag as he had expected, but quite a sweet looking little old lady, with white hair done in a neat bun and glasses slipping down her nose.

She didn't seem to notice him at first, but bent to welcome the black cat, which had run ahead to rub against her with its back arched.

"There's my pretty little puss!" said the witch. She didn't cackle at all – in fact, her voice was quite gentle. "Come home to Mother, have you? That's right! And what have you brought me?"

The cat put something into her hand from its mouth.

"Oh, *nasty*!" she cried. "Naughty Ackerbackus! You *know* Mother doesn't use toads. Poor little thing," she said to the toad. Midas thought she chucked it under the chin. "Don't be frightened, Ackerbackus shall take you home."

She gave it back to the cat, who went off rather sulkily.

"Straight back where you found him!" the witch called after it sternly.

Then she saw the King, and smiled vaguely at him.

"I'm so sorry I didn't hear you come in," she said. "I'm rather hard of hearing." She straightened the frilly apron she wore over her lavender dress and patted her hair. "You must excuse my cat. He used to work for one of the old-fashioned *wicked* witches, and he can't get used to the fact that I don't employ black magic. He will keep bringing me bats and snails and things . . . Only last week, he came home with a leopard's liver! Imagine! I can't think where he found it . . ."

She shook her head indulgently.

"Oh dear me," she added, "I'm such a Mrs Thoughtless! Chattering away when you must be tired. Do come and sit down." She beckoned him to a high-backed wooden chair by the fire.

He was, indeed, very tired, and chilled to the bone from the damp tunnels. He stumbled forward. The old lady was standing beside the chair, patting the seat of it invitingly, but as he drew near it, he hesitated.

It was carved all over with strange, evil-looking creatures: spiders, snakes, monkeys, lizards, and others he couldn't gives names to, all very lifelike and with mean, demonic little faces. The firelight made their eyes gleam as if they were alive.

"You mustn't be afraid of my chair," said the old lady. "It's very old, you know. I keep it as a conversation-piece! Will you take some tea? Indian, or China?"

The King was reassured, and sat down in the chair, which was so extraordinarily comfortable that he felt as if he never wanted to get up from it. In fact, he was suddenly so comfortable, and felt so much at home, that he somehow felt he could tell this kind old lady everything that led up to the fact that he couldn't "take tea", much as he would have liked some.

She listened with great sympathy, nodding and tut-tutting every now and then until he came to the part about the mumbo.

"Oh, that naughty boy!" she exclaimed. "Up to his tricks . . . How many times have I told him he mustn't frighten my visitors!" She gave him a quaint little smile. "Turned him into gold, did you?" she said. "Oh, that was clever. That was *extremely* clever!"

"It was nothing, really," murmured the King, puffing out his chest.

The witch seemed to think for a moment, and then said, "But you'll be wanting your tea. Now don't worry – I can give it to you, you won't have to touch the cup."

She lifted one down from a hook above the fire. It was black. Midas had never seen a black cup before, and somehow it alarmed him. He straightened up, away from the back of the chair, and it came to him that he'd come here looking for something, something that had gone entirely out of his head the moment he entered the cave. What was it?

He gazed round the cave with a puzzled frown. His eyes stopped on some irregular shape he could just make out, in a dark corner, but before he could think about what it might be, the old lady, who had been ladling some tea out of the cauldron with a long-handled spoon, came towards him.

"Funny way to serve tea," thought Midas. "Perhaps she doesn't have a tea-pot."

The sound of the pouring tea was still in his ears. It reminded him of something. Pouring . . . trickling . . . Water! That was it! Old Gollop – he'd *forgotten* Old Gollop!

"Flandy-bakes!" he exclaimed suddenly.

"What?" asked the witch rather sharply.

"I came to find the flandy-bake tree to help unblock the River Cijam."

"Yes," she said smilingly. "I know. Mother knows all about it. Now drink your nice hot tea." And she put the cup temptingly against his lower lip.

The smell of the tea was irresistible, the old lady's face bland and reassuring, but Midas was not entirely easy in his mind.

"But what about my hands?"

"You need not bother about Gollop and his second-rate magic. Right after tea, I shall unspell your hands. Drink up now."

"Is there sugar in it?" asked Midas with a little gulp.

"Ah! You have a sweet tooth!" she said indulgently. "I have something *very* special for that!"

She moved into the dark corner Midas had been peering into before. When she turned round, she had a strange thing in her hand, a large lump of something marked with pink and white stripes.

She cracked it gently on the edge of her cauldron and broke a small chip off it which she dropped in the cup.

"This will do your cold good, too," she said.

"What is it?"

"Something nice. Drink up!" she coaxed.

The King's eyes were getting used to the dark, and now he could see, in the corner, a little tree growing in a pot. It wasn't like any other tree the King had ever seen. It had gnarled, spreading branches covered with furry grey moss, and more of the strange fruits looking like pink-striped candy the size of his fist.

"Is that a flandy-bake tree?" asked the King.

"A what?" asked the witch sharply, looking round. "Oh, no, no, no! Whatever made you think that? That's a blundernut bush. Come along now, drink up your tea while it's hot."

But something in her manner, when he'd mentioned the flandy-bakes, made him hesitate.

"Er – are you sure this tea is – all right?"

The witch drew back. Tears came to her eyes.

"It's not fair," she said, with heartfelt sincerity. "Just because I'm a witch, you think I'm untrustworthy. It's witchism, that's what it is! You're prejudiced against witches!"

"I assure you, I'm the most unprejudiced man alive!" said the King. "I judge everyone according to how they treat me!"

"And haven't I treated you well?" she murmured, wiping her old eyes with a lace hanky.

The sight of her tears sent a pang of remorse through Midas. Hadn't he caused enough hurt? All doubts fled.

"Yes, you have! Oh, please don't cry!" said the King. "I'll drink your tea at once, I'm dying for some!"

She lifted the cup again to his lips. He drank its contents to the last drop.

"Excellent cuppa, that," he said. "Would you be kind enough to – to wipe my moustache?"

She obliged him, and then said, rather oddly, "You'll soon feel better. Shall we have another log on the fire?"

She threw on a funny, twisted log and sat on a high stool. She said nothing more, but sat quite still, with her hands folded, as if waiting for something.

The light in the cave seemed to have faded, and the King noticed that the fire was now burning with blue and green flames, as if she had thrown tinsel on it. Strange black smoke began to drift into the room. Everything grew darker and darker.

"Er – your fire's smoking," said the King, giving a little cough. But the witch just sat there with the blackness swirling round her.

The King was feeling oddly sleepy, but when he closed his eyes, his head spun and he opened them again with an effort.

What he saw made him wonder if he *had* fallen asleep and was having a ghastly nightmare.

The witch had changed.

Her nose was long and warty, and curved to her chin. Her hair straggled out from under a pointed black hat. Her lavender dress had changed to wild tatters. On her knee sat Ackerbackus the black cat, with a newt in his mouth, and the witch was stroking him with long, bony hands. Her nails were green.

Her eyes – awful, malevolent eyes – were fixed on him. When she saw his expression, she threw back her head and gave a dreadful cackle of spine-freezing laughter before the black smoke swallowed her completely, and King Midas fell into a deep, unnatural sleep.

Chapter Seven

The Mumbo

When the King next opened his eyes, he wasn't sure at first whether he'd opened them or not, because it was almost completely dark. Then he saw a tiny glow from the embers of the fire, and instantly he remembered everything.

He tried to jump out of his chair, but as he did so, he heard dozens of little hissing voices, like the sea on shingle, whispering:

"You can't move! *You can't move!*"

And sure enough, he found he couldn't. There was nothing to do but sit still and think. His thoughts were not very pleasant.

He had let the old witch trick him good and proper.

"Is there no end to my folly, my – my gullibility?" he groaned aloud.

"You are good at long words, aren't you?"

asked a familiar voice in the darkness. "Your what, did you say?"

The King gasped. The mumbo! Here! And no longer gold! Hope – hope was here, too, and it made the King feel weak and then suddenly strong.

He tried to carry on a normal conversation, over the wild beating of his heart.

"Gullible," he remarked, "means easily taken in or tricked."

"And that's you?"

"That's me all right," said the King.

"You weren't being very gullible when you turned me into gold," said the mumbo. "Not very nice, either."

"Indeed! And no doubt you consider it very nice to threaten to eat people who've never done you any harm?"

"Only joking," said the mumbo crossly. "I can't eat people yet. I've lost most of my baby teeth and I haven't got my proper ones. I was only going to gnaw on you a bit," it went on in an injured tone. "There was no need to turn me into gold."

"What did it feel like, when you were gold?" asked the King.

"It was the most nastiest horriblest miserablest frozenest feeling, all cold and . . . See how I'm using my longest words and I still can't describe it! I wouldn't do it to anyone. Not even *her*."

"Her? Who?" asked the King quickly.

"No one," said the mumbo.

"How did you – I mean, who changed you back?"

"She did."

"She? Her? The witch?"

"Of course. She needed me to guard you while she's off on her rotten old broomstick." He yawned loudly. "She's been gone for hours, and I'm bored out of my scales. I thought you'd never wake up and talk to me."

The King said cautiously, "Don't you like her?"

There was a long pause. Then the King felt that hot, smoky breath on his ear.

"Can't stand her!"

"Why?"

"She is so mean, you can't imagine. Would you believe that after stealing Gollop's flandy-bake tree, that he used to let me help myself from – it grew right next to him in case his throat ever got blocked up – saying she wanted it to feed *me*, she won't even give me one fruit off it? She makes me eat the most disgusting messes she cooks up in that cauldron of hers, right on top of all kinds of spelling potions, yucky isn't the word! I swallowed half a rat yesterday ... Ugh! I was as sick as a parrot."

"But you said when you've got your proper teeth you'll be eating people," said the King. "You can't be exactly a vegetarian."

There was another pause, and then the mumbo muttered, "Well, let's just say I'm told I'm meant to eat people when I'm bigger. I can't actually imagine myself doing it, if you want the truth. All I really like is flandy-bakes, especially toasted. I wish I had one now!"

The King said, "Well, look over there, there's a whole tree laden with them."

"Where?!" cried the mumbo eagerly.

"Over there somewhere, I saw it before I drank that so-called tea."

"Oh," said the mumbo, lapsing into gloom. "That one. That's the one I've been talking about. She pulled it out of its pot by the roots before she went off, and took it with her, so I couldn't nick any. I tell you, she's the meannest cruellest starvingest —"

"You know, those aren't all real words," mentioned Midas. "If you wanted to know some real long words, I could teach you some."

"Like stackalite and gullabubble?"

"Er – yes."

"But it's no use. I can't learn anything while I'm so hungry."

"Why don't you just run away?" asked the King.

"Nowhere else to go," explained the mumbo sadly. "She stole me from my mother as soon as I was hatched. If I went out into the world, people would chase me and kill me. I've got no one to look after me."

There was a long, painful silence. Midas had no idea whether mumbos could cry, but this one sounded as if he felt quite bad enough to, if he could. He felt another rash impulse coming on that he couldn't resist.

"Listen, Mumbo," said the King. "If you'll help me get out of this place, and to get unmagicked, you can come and live with me at my palace, and no one shall hurt you. I promise."

The moment the words were out of his mouth, the King regretted them. He'd never even seen this creature, and the notion he had had of him as a huge black balloon-monster with a terrifying face was still with him. But it was too late now. His word, as they say, had gone from him.

"No one keeps promises," mumbled the mumbo.

"I do," said the King. "All the best kings do."

"Are you a real king?"

"Yes. And I've given you my word. Now, what about some help?"

"All right," said the mumbo. "It couldn't be worse than living with *her*. What do you want first?"

"I can't seem to move out of this chair," said the King.

"You're being gubblullable again."

"Gullible," corrected the King. "What do you mean?"

"You can get up when you want to. All those little horrors on the chair just have you tricked into thinking you can't."

The King again tried to get up.

"You can't move! You can't MOVE!" shrieked the villainous little voices frantically.

"Of course he can," said the mumbo. "Shut your ugly faces, you little beasts, or I'll throw you in the fire, chair and all!"

The voices gave hissing cries of protest and then died away into silence. The King stood up easily.

"Could we have some more light?" asked the King, who could hardly wait to see what he had invited into his home.

"There's some stuff Wuzzy throws onto the fire to make it burn brightly," said the mumbo. The King could hear him fumbling among the jars and bottles on the mantlepiece.

"Let's try this."

There was a sudden burst of white flame that made the cave as bright as day.

The King gave a gasp of astonishment. "It can't be!" he thought. But it was. Right there in front of his eyes.

The mumbo looked rather like a large green kangaroo, only with hands and feet like a squirrel's and a spiked tail. A fat stomach, a soft dappled green skin with scales on the back, small leathery wings . . .

"You – you're a *dragon*!" he exclaimed, aghast.

"Of course," said the mumbo. "I'm a mumbo. That's what you call a baby dragon, like a kitten is a baby cat and a puppy is a baby dog. Fancy you with all your long words, not knowing a thing like that!"

"But dragons are – well, to say the least, very rare, if not completely extinct!" ("Ex-TINK-t! Ex-TINK-t!" echoed the mumbo gleefully.) "Of course I've heard the rumours that there are a few surviving in the mountains, but I've certainly never heard of anyone seeing one!"

"If anyone did see one, what do you think would happen?"

"Ah. You mean – hunters, zoologists, sight-seers, all that?"

"My mother didn't have time to teach me anything, but never mind EX-tinks, I have my INstinks, and they tell me to keep well out of sight. That's why I've stuck it here with Wuzzleflump all my life. Are you sure I'll be safe in your palace?"

"I shall see to it that you are. IF we can escape. But before we do, there's something very important I have to know. How did the witch take the golden spell off you?"

"It must have been something she mixed up specially. Let's look in the cauldron. She's revoltingly untidy, she never cleans it out till she needs it for something else, not always then."

They looked inside the blackened pot. There was a strange purple mixture bubbling in the bottom.

"That's it!" said the Mumbo. "She must have sprinkled me with it. I wiped some off my ears when I woke up."

"Let's take it! I'll need every drop!" cried the King, the hope now blazing in his heart. This was it! This was what he needed to bring all the things he'd touched back to life – to save Delia! He felt inclined to forgive the witch everything, just for her carelessness in leaving these dregs behind!

The mumbo found an empty bottle and carefully ladled into it all that was left of the precious purple liquid. Just as he put the top on, he let out a bellow.

"Ouch, it's hot!"

And he flung it from him.

The King didn't have time to think. His right hand snapped out and caught the bottle as it flew through the air.

It didn't burn him, of course, because hot bottle and hot life-saving fluid turned, as one, into gold.

"You great gubblabooby!" yelled the Mumbo jumping up and down, entirely forgetting whose fault it was.

They peered into the cauldron, and on all sides of the ladle, but both were quite magically spotless.

"This can't be happening!" cried the King despairingly. "I can't bear it!"

"What does that mean?" asked the mumbo interestedly. "If it's not happening, what is happening, and if you can't bear it, what will you do instead?"

That brought the King to his senses. After all, there was no real alternative to bearing it.

"All right, I'll bear it. But we must think."

They both thought hard. Suddenly the King

said, "Your ears! You said it was all over your ears!"

"Yes! But I wiped it off."

"Then it's on your paws!"

The mumbo stretched out his squirrel-like paws. Both were stained purple!

"Touch the bottle! Rub it, rub the stuff onto it!" cried the King.

The Mumbo took the golden bottle in his paws and rubbed it hard.

Nothing.

"It's dried!"

"Lick it! Lick the stain!"

"Must I? Yuck . . ."

But the mumbo did lick both his paws with a long forked tongue, and then rubbed again. It worked! Not perfectly, but enough so that the bottle became a bottle and the purple liquid around the outside was restored. In the middle of the bottle was still a great lump of unrestored gold; but as the mumbo shook the bottle and the purple liquid circulated, the gold slowly dissolved.

"Oh, thank heaven!" cried the King. "Quick! Slip it in my pocket – no, the back one, where I'm not so likely to touch it by mistake!"

The mumbo, squeaking with excitement, did as he was told.

"Now, quickly, we must go, before she comes back!"

"I know a secret back way out – this way—"

The King hurried towards the mumbo, who

was standing in a nook by the fireplace. Suddenly he put his foot on something like a round stone, turned his ankle, and fell. The flagstone under his hand turned to gold; but the King hardly noticed. The Mumbo had swooped upon the thing he'd trodden on and was dancing with delight.

"It's a FLANDY-BAKE! – Oh, and look, look! There's another! She must have dropped them when she pulled up the tree!"

The mumbo turned, clutching in each front paw a large, striped lump. He was grinning and panting like a dog. Then he opened his mouth and was just going to pop one of the lumps in when the King cried: "Stop!"

"Why?"

"Listen! This purple stuff won't take the spell off my hands! Only Old Gollop can do that, and to do it he needs at least one of those flandy-bake things. You must save one for him – otherwise, even if I take you home with me, I'll never be able to touch you, and I shall probably soon starve to death."

"I'm starving to death now!" said the mumbo, opening his mouth very wide again.

"Oh, don't, pray don't!" cried the King.

"You only need one for Gollop, so why can't I eat the other one?"

"If we had one, we could plant it, and grow a tree from it in my greenhouse. Otherwise I really don't know what I'm going to feed you on."

The mumbo lowered his paw. "And what am I going to eat till it grows?" he asked. "Lumpy porridge thickened with dead rats, I suppose, like I get here."

"Put them into my side pockets," said the King. Huffing rebelliously through his large nostrils, the mumbo obeyed.

Just at that moment there was a loud *too-whoo* from the snow-white owl, which made the King shiver.

"Quick! That means she's coming!" whispered the mumbo. "Out the back way!"

He pressed a knob on the rock, and a section of it opened out silently, revealing a secret passage. They were just going to dive into it, when from the carved chair came the hiss of the evil little creatures: "She'll get you! She'll get you!"

"They'll tell and she'll be after us in two seconds!" said the mumbo in a frightened whisper.

"Not if I know it!" said the King, and, running back, he touched the chair.

"She won't be able to change it back till she's mixed up another brew!" he said as they closed the secret door behind them and hurried along the passage.

Chapter Eight

Flight By Moonlight

*T*he King stumbled after the mumbo for a long way through the pitch-dark, winding tunnel.

"Ouch!" he exclaimed, banging his nose on a stalactite. "I wish you'd remember I can't see in the dark!"

"Oh! Sorry. Is this better?"

The mumbo appeared in the darkness, by some light of his own. He glowed a faint green, growing brighter towards his chest, which glowed red.

"You're luminous!" exclaimed the King admiringly. "How do you do that?" (They were both talking in whispers.)

"I can only *just* do it," he whispered back, "now I'm bigger and the fire in my lungs is starting to form. Soon I'll be able to breathe flames!"

He huffed and puffed a bit, making noises like a bellows, and the red glow in his chest got brighter, but all he could manage was a few puffs of smoke. "Then I'll be able to toast my own flandy-bakes!" he added proudly. "Come on then, don't hang about!"

They could both go faster after that, and soon they smelt clean, fresh air. There was no daylight, though, and the King realised he had slept until the middle of the night.

"Sh! Don't make a sound!" muttered the mumbo as they emerged cautiously from the back entrance to the cave. "She might be anywhere!"

"Can she make herself invisible?"

"She can if she likes, but she probably won't bother. She'll just be flying overhead, looking for us."

"Lucky it's night!"

"We could do without the moon, though."

There was a nearly-full moon hanging in the night sky. Midas hadn't noticed it at first because they were in a forest.

"She can't see us through these trees, can she?"

"I wouldn't bet on it. She's full of tricks. Look out! – There she is!"

The King looked up. Silhouetted for a moment against the moon he saw a horrid sight: the witch, sailing through the sky on her broomstick, with Ackerbackus riding on the twigs behind her. The mumbo and the King crouched in the deep shadow of a large tree and watched her swooping down again and again over the forest canopy.

"Turn off your luminosity!" hissed the King suddenly.

"Oh, what a lovely word! Loo-min – Oh!" Realising, he faded his glow, and not a moment too soon.

Down out of the sky right above them Wuzzleflump's broomstick swooped. As it flattened out just above the tree-tops, so close they could hear the whistle of the wind in the twigs, her cracked voice screeched:

"We'll find 'em, Ackerbackus! We'll find 'em if it takes us all night long! And when we do, we'll turn 'em into we-e-e-eazles!"

And she whooshed up towards the moon again.

As soon as she'd gone – for the moment – the mumbo urged the King onward. Following him from shadow to shadow, from tree to tree, Midas felt they were getting near the edge of the wood and the beginning of the rocks where Old Gollop lived. "We're going to make it!" he thought. "We're going to –"

But abruptly, without warning, a faint meow from above froze them into stillness.

She wasn't directly above their heads, but some distance away, her broomstick hovering like a kestrel. Yet her voice, now a singsong whine, seemed to sound right in their ears:

"King's right hand that belongs to me,
Reach out now and touch a tree!"

It happened before the King could even think of stopping it. His right hand shot out without his bidding, and laid itself upon the trunk of the nearest tree.

It was a tall pine. Instantly it became a golden beacon, an arrow, shining in the moonlight, pointing directly to the spot where they stood!

The witch put her broomstick into a steep dive.

The King, despite his panic, knew he must act quickly. Running out from under the golden pine, he touched another tree, and another, in a widening circle around the tree he had touched first. There was an island of golden trees in the midst of the forest.

All he had meant to do was confuse the witch as to which tree they were sheltering under. But his quick thinking did better than that.

In mid-air the witch tried to alter course, pointing the broom-handle first this way, then that, as tree after tree flashed golden in the moonlight. Suddenly she lost control and crash-dived straight onto a vast golden beech-tree.

It was a hard landing! It made a terrific noise, compounded of the loud rattle of golden leaves, the clash of branches, the snapping of the broomstick, the yowl of the cat and the shrieks and curses of the witch.

"Great stuff! Maybe you've killed her! Let's get out of here!"

They rushed pell-mell out of the forest and began scrambling up among the rocks by the dried river bed. Once, they turned and looked back. The golden "umbrella" of trees showed up clearly among the other dark treetops. There was a broken area where the witch had crashed, but they couldn't see any sign of her.

"I didn't think you could kill a witch," panted the King, who was making heavy weather of the climb. "Not just like that, anyhow."

"You could be right," said the mumbo. "She's always boasting that she'll live for ever. But another witch she knew died once, or 'was no more' as she called it. She was furious about it, kept saying she should have known better. So there's got to be a way."

The King was dredging his mind for every bit of folklore he'd ever heard about witches.

"I read once . . ." he began.

"Save your breath, King, and climb!" the mumbo interrupted. "We're nearly there!"

"Can't you fly? You've got wings!" asked the King as he struggled upward in the mumbo's wake.

"They're still too small to lift me! But just wait till I'm a bit older, I'll be able to fly as well as any stupid old broomstick!"

It wasn't much longer before they came out into Old Gollop's clearing, and there he was, fast asleep, with not a trickle of water coming out of his mouth.

"Wake up, Mr Gollop, sir!" said the mumbo,

throwing his weight against the side of the rock. "We've brought you a flandy-bake to clear your throat."

"Hm? Hah? Grrrump?" wheezed Old Gollop.

"He can't talk at all," said the King. "Take one out of my pocket and put it in his mouth! We've got to get the river flowing again!"

The Mumbo obeyed.

"Grrrunfff ... gluggle ... d'licious ..." mumbled the old boulder.

What happened next was like an old mill-wheel starting, slowly, to turn as the water strikes its paddles, the cogs squeak into action and the axles begin to turn the millstones. There was a faint splashing, some knocking sounds, some deep rumblings, and then a steady grinding while the watery sounds grew louder.

All at once the rocky mouth twisted into something like a smile, and at the same moment, with a rushing and a bubbling, water gushed out, fresh and clean and cold. It filled the rock basin under Old Gollop's chin, overflowed down the first waterfall, and went pouring and chattering over the rocks below and down the hillside.

Hardly had this happened when the King felt a shadow cross the moon. He looked up in fearful apprehension, and saw her – her broomstick renewed, the cat in its place, and the witch, quite unhurt – diving straight at them!

"She's seen the moon on the water!" burbled

Gollop wetly. "Quick! Hold onto my nose and jump into the pool under my chin!"

They grabbed the big stony nose and jumped, and were knee-deep in Cijam water by the time she swooshed down and landed on the river bank, so fast that the handle of her broom dug a long runnel in the grass.

The King didn't know what to expect, other than the worst. The pool was only a few yards wide. The witch, even without magic, could have reached out her skinny arms and grabbed them both. But she didn't.

Keeping well back from the edge of the pool, she went into contortions. She hurled herself about, she jumped, she twirled, she flung her twisted green-nailed fingers at them in furious gestures. She shouted and screamed, uttering spells in every magic language. The King had never seen anyone so angry – not even himself in a rage! She was beside herself. But it didn't do her any good at all.

The King, who had been wincing and ducking every time he thought a spell was heading his way, noticed that the mumbo was standing beside him perfectly calmly.

"Why can't she do anything to us?" the King muttered in the mumbo's ear.

"Oh, it's the water of course," said the mumbo. "Witches can't bear water at all."

"Ah!" breathed the King. "That's what I remember reading!"

"There was no water in that tea you drank,

it was all pure spelling-fluid. She hasn't a drop of water in her body, it's all horrible smelly green gunge. And now look at her, going mad because she can't send spells across even a few inches of it!"

"That's because this water's special," burbled Gollop. "It's her enemy. That's why she stole my flandy-bakes, and why she keeps blocking my throat ... You're safe as long as you stand there."

"But how long can we stand here? I'm getting so cold!" said Midas.

"Cold, are you!" shrieked Wuzzleflump. "That's nothing to what you'll be when I get my hands on you! I'll shut you up in blocks of ice! I'll hang you upside-down in snowdrifts, for ever, do you hear me? How dare you defy me? How dare you make a fool of me? I haven't crashed my broomstick since I was a novice!"

The mumbo sniggered rudely. "Bet that was a good few years ago!"

"As for *you*," she said with bitter fury, "You, that I nurtured from the moment you hatched, that I treated as my own, that I lavished good food on—"

"Good food! That's a laugh!" sneered the Mumbo. "Your leftovers, more like – thanks for nothing, Wuzzy!" And he tried to splash her. She leapt back.

"You disloyal, deceitful little – *human*!" she screamed. (Midas understood this was a term of abuse, like a person calling someone a beast.)

"You will regret this treachery! I will *disdragon* you! I will clip your wings! I will draw your teeth one by one as they emerge so you will never taste man's flesh! And you will never breathe fire, for I shall put it out for ever! I will see you grovel at my feet for the dregs of my pot, you wretched little ingrate, I will make you my helpless slave!"

As she uttered these terrible threats, she was moving closer and closer, her body twisting and writhing, her snaggle-teeth bared, her green eyes fastened hypnotically on the mumbo. Midas saw to his horror that the mumbo's paws were growing slack, loosing their hold on the rocky nose. Her threats were frightening him without magic until he lost his will.

"Mumbo! Don't listen!" the King cried.

But the mumbo was slipping, slipping – another moment, and the tumbling water would sweep him down to his doom!

The King once again forgot his curse. Just as the mumbo was about to be carried over the edge, Midas's hand shot out and grasped the mumbo's paw.

Chapter Nine

"Gone For Ever!"

They stared at each other as the witch raved on, and the water rushed past, tugging at their legs.

"You saved me!" said the mumbo.

"I *touched* you," said the King. "And you're still you."

"Of course," rumbled Gollop. "Your hands got wet where the water first comes out of my mouth. The spell is broken. Your curse is removed."

"Oh, thank you! Thank you!" cried the King ecstatically. He actually kissed Old Gollop's nose, and then heaved the mumbo back from the brink and hugged him, nearly causing them both to be swept away. The witch was so astounded by these goings-on that she stopped in the midst of her rantings.

"What are you so happy about?" she snarled.

"Oh! I know! You've lost the golden touch! Well, don't rejoice too soon – I can soon put that back. Nandan isn't the only one who knows that trick! Not by a tall hat, he isn't!"

"You've got to get at us first!" taunted the mumbo.

"No," thought Midas. "We have got to get at her."

Shivering from the cold, he crouched down, allowing the magic waters to pour all over him from his head downwards till he was completely soaked. Then he straightened up and, disguising his quaking terror, waded boldly out of the pool on the witch's side and faced her.

She couldn't believe her eyes as she saw him coming. As he put his foot on the bank, streaming with Cijam water, she moved uncontrollably backward, away from him, her hands warding him off.

"You dare – you dare –!" she spluttered. But there was fear in her face.

"Get out of the pool on the other side, mumbo," ordered the King without looking round. He heard the mumbo splashing behind him. Then, keeping his eyes fixed on the witch's glowing green ones, he counted three, nerved himself with a deep breath, and seized her.

The King felt her bony shoulders shrink from his grip, then go squashy, then seem to dissolve away so that his fists clenched on emptiness. She snatched herself from his grasp. The King gasped. *There were holes in her shoulders where his hands had been.*

She backed away, her face savage with rage and dread. The King advanced, she backed faster, until – suddenly a yowl filled the night.

She had trodden on Ackerbackus!

The black cat, every hair on end, burst from under her feet and clawed the backs of her legs, sending her stumbling forward right into the King's wet arms.

The King wasted no time. In a second she would have melted free of him again. Holding the detestable bundle of rags and wickedness, he spun round to face the river, and, while she was still off balance, hurled her into it.

The shriek she uttered as she hit the water was so piercing it echoed to the farthest corners of the kingdom, making people miles away start from their sleep.

By some last exertion of power, she bounced off the surface and shot straight into the air, and the King thought his plan had failed. But for Wuzzleflump it was too late. The water had touched her.

As her flying figure reached its peak, it changed. The rags she wore, and her pointed hat, made a ragged star-shape spread against the moon, blotting it out for a moment. There was a sudden deadness in the air, like an explosion in reverse, a complete absence of sound. And then a tatty bundle of black rags and an old dented hat fluttered into the pool, turned slowly once, and were washed over the rim.

Gone.

"She is no more!" shouted the mumbo from the other side. "She should have known better! Oh King, you're so brave, you're so clever! Give me some good, long words to tell you how brave and clever you are or I shall burst!"

"Extremelyfortunate," said the King. "Providentiallylucky."

"Yum, yum, lovely!" slurped the mumbo. "Only I know I shall forget them in a minute! You're the extremelyfortunatest and providentiallyluckiest king in the world!"

"Where's that cat?" asked Midas, who was still feeling very shaky and completely unbrave and unclever. "Acky-backy or whatever your name is, come out!"

A pathetic, straggly little form crawled out from under a rock, crept along the ground and rubbed itself humbly against Midas's wet trouser-leg. When it didn't blow up or melt away, Midas realised at once that it wasn't very wicked and had no magic powers of its own. He bent down to stroke it. It felt pitifully thin.

"I don't think she fed this one much either," Midas said. "You were a great help, you know, Acky-backy. I think you'd better come home with us. Heavens! How good it is to stroke a cat's soft fur and have it stay that way!"

Then he and the mumbo turned to thank Old Gollop. There just didn't seem to be any words that would do the job adequately.

The mumbo turned to the King.

"Would I be a little bit strexstremilynorfanate,

too, if I said, let's give him the other flandy-bake? I don't mind – much – eating porridge for the rest of my life, now you're all right again."

So they set off for home, the three of them.

The King was so relieved to be able to touch things without turning them into gold that he almost danced ahead, doing it just for fun. He was far more happy and excited by what *didn't* happen than he had been (except just at first) by what did, when he had used his magic gift.

The mumbo shuffled along behind talking in cat-language to Acky-backy (they had become friends and allies while half-starving together with the witch), and trying not to think about flandy-bakes. It had felt great when he gave up his last flandy-bake to Gollop, and the King had given him a new long word all of his own, saying how totally, wondrously *self-sacrificing* he was being; but now he was thinking that being *that*, as well as extremelyfortunate, had its drawbacks.

No flandy-bake to plant, no flandy-bake tree coming along to feed him in his new life . . . No flandy-bakes, ever again. He didn't regret what he'd done, but he did wonder if he'd do it again now, if he had the chance over again, the last delicious ripe striped sweet-sour-solid crunchy munchy mouth-melting satisfying flandy-bake here in his paw . . .

"Mumbo! Look there!"

They were passing the seventh waterfall on

their climb down to the valley. The mumbo looked, looked again, goggled – and pounced!

There, lying abandoned beside the seventh waterfall, with its torn-up roots in the air, and many of its fruits scattered on the ground, was – the flandy-bake tree!

"Mine, all mine!" he cried, stuffing two into his mouth at once and sending big stripy flakes flying in all directions. "And here's the tree, too! She must have just dumped it there! We can take it back and plant it in your garden and not have to wait while a new one grows! Here, you try one!"

He handed a lump the size of a grapefruit to Midas.

Only now, looking at this wonderful object and smelling its mysterious, mouth-watering smell, did the King realise that he hadn't eaten properly for nearly two days. He held it in both hands and took a huge bite. His teeth sank into it, a large piece filled his mouth and he chewed and chewed . . .

After a long time, he swallowed it down. A look of bliss was on his face.

"That," he said, "is the most delicious thing I have ever tasted in my life. It's got all the good tastes in the world wrapped up in one thing." He handed the rest of it back. "But that's all I want. One bite has satisfied me . . . Amazing!"

"It is amazing," said the mumbo, stuffing down the King's flandy-bake. "One never satisfies me! Oh, this is just so . . . Give me a word, quick!"

"Palatable, delectable, toothsome, luscious—"

"Too short! Not long enough!" he cried, jumping up and down.

"Superscrumptious, how's that?"

"Perfect! Scrooperumpshus! Love it! You are such a clever King!"

"I'm a silly old dimwit, is what I am," said Midas ruefully. "What's that cat doing?"

"Eating the bits."

"Oh! Do cats like it, too?"

"Everything likes flandy-bakes," said the mumbo.

"Princesses, too?"

"I don't know, but I bet. Why, do you know one?"

"You could say so."

"Is there a story?"

So the King, as they walked along, carrying the tree between them, told the mumbo (who told the cat in translation) the whole story. Acky-backy couldn't understand a word of it. The mumbo found it rather difficult, as well . . .

"You mean, you wanted everything to be made of gold? Everything to be the *same*?" he kept asking incredulously.

"I know now how foolish it was. Nothing in the world suits everybody."

"Of course not, think how boring!"

"Though some people think everyone should *believe* the same," said Midas thoughtfully.

"What I believe is only suitable for mumbos," said the mumbo firmly.

"What do you believe?"

"That mumbos should have plenty of flandy-bakes to eat and grow up to be dragons and fly and breathe fire and—"

"—Eat people?"

The mumbo didn't answer at first. "Wouldn't eat you, anyhow," he muttered at last.

"What about my little daughter?"

"Depends. If she's very tasty, I might fancy her. It's my nature, after all," he added.

The King said nothing. He was frowning.

It was quite light by this time, and when they came to the field at the foot of the hills, there stood the cow, with the first sunlight shining on her golden horns.

The King took out the witch's purple antidote, dipped one finger into it, and, holding his breath, smeared it on her forehead.

The magic charm worked instantly. The King thought he had never seen anything so beautiful as the glossy black-and-white patches on her hide, and her gentle brown eyes as she turned to look at him.

"Is this her?" asked the mumbo.

"Pardon?"

"Is this the princess? Because if so, you needn't worry, I shan't fancy eating her."

"This, my dear Mumbo, is A Cow," explained the King rather testily. "My daughter is *not* A Cow, she is a beautiful little girl. On two legs. Like me."

"Oh," said the mumbo.

They went on their way, the King shaking his head. He was extremely fond of the mumbo by now, after all they'd been through together, but it couldn't be denied that he was feeling rather worried.

"How – er, how *large* do you think you might get, when you're – er – fully grown-up and a dragon?" he asked, trying to sound careless.

"Oh, I shall be absolutely gi-normous," said the mumbo cheerfully.

"Gi-normous? What kind of word is that?"

"It's my word, that I made up. It means, very large."

"So I guessed," said the King gloomily.

But he couldn't stay gloomy for long. Soon the palace came in sight and the King, unable to contain himself, began to run.

His heart was beating very hard. Delia was there ahead of him. He felt he was running towards her – her coldness, her miserableness, all the things about being gold that the mumbo had said. He was running swiftly to relieve all that, to bring her back to herself. Oh, when he could gather her in his arms, take her on his knee, tell her all his adventures – tell her he was sorry! Only then would the nightmare really be over!

There were no gardeners in the garden, no cooks in the kitchen, no housemaids in the scullery and no footmen in the long halls. Momentarily puzzled, the King paused, then remembered. Of course! All the servants except the faithful Biffpot had abandoned him.

The King wasted no more time, but panted up the marble stairway as fast as he could. The purple charm still clinging to his fingers turned the banisters back into carved oak, but he didn't notice. He ran along the passage, with the mumbo and the cat behind him, in through the golden door of his room. There he stopped dead.

The golden pillow was there, and the golden bell, and there stood the golden screen. But there was no sign of Biffpot, and when the King, with foreboding clutching his heart, pulled the screen aside – Delia wasn't there.

The King's hope had been so high and sure, his happiness so near, that this final blow brought him to his knees. He buried his face in his hands.

"What's wrong? What's happened?" cried the mumbo, while the cat rubbed its head against Midas's knee.

The King did not look up. He was sunk to his lowest.

"She's gone," he groaned. "The witch must have come for her while I slept. I have lost her. She is gone for ever."

Chapter Ten

Under the Palace

"**I** don't believe this," said the mumbo. "You can't give up, not now! Not an astreemly-nortunate man like you."

The King shook his head brokenly, still on his knees on the floor.

"I am not extremely fortunate at all, not in any sense," he muttered. "I am the most wretched, the most cursed of men! Gone from me, stolen, my dearest treasure on this earth – and the only one who could tell me where she is – is *no more!*"

He let out a terrible groan of despair.

"Oh, do get up," said the mumbo impatiently. "I don't believe Wuzzy had time to get here and do anything to your princess, and if she did, she can't have taken her far – a great golden statue, on her broomstick, come *on!*"

The King stopped groaning and raised his head a little.

"But she could have cast a spell on her – or taken the spell off – or killed her – oh no – my darling –" And the poor man broke down again in tears.

The mumbo contemplated him for a moment.

"I don't think you're as streemly-whatsit as I thought," he said disgustedly. "Why don't you think a little, if you're so provi-whoosit? Who do you think went with her on her broomstick, who can tell us everything, and that's right here rubbing all his silly fur off against your big fat head?"

The King slowly reached one of his hands out from under his face, which was practically on the carpet, and felt around with his fingers till he touched something soft, warm and furry. As soon as he did, he jerked upright.

"The cat! Of course! What a dismal old fool I am! Well, don't stand there, Mumbo – ask him!"

Mumbo starting making meowing noises, and the cat answered. The King jumped to his feet and wrung his hands in impatience.

"Well? Well? What does he say? Did they come here?"

"Yes," reported the mumbo. "They came. They came right into this room. There was a big golden statue here, and a little man with a pointed nose who fell down in a faint at the sight of Wuzzy."

"Fell down in a faint!"

"Don't be too rough on him, she probably did her turn-you-to-jelly-if-you-look-at-me bit.

Anyway then she worked a spell so that the statue got light enough for her to carry, and she was just going to load it onto the broomstick when the owl hooted."

"What owl? Not the one in her cave?"

"Yes. She could hear it at any distance, and it warned her that we were about to escape. She was furious. She said –" He stopped. "Well, I'd rather not repeat it. I'm afraid Acky learnt some rather bad words from the witch, but anyway she left everything here and leapt back on her broomstick – Acky says he barely scrambled on in time – and zoomed away, threatening to return as soon as she'd settled our hash. But then we settled hers instead."

"So where's my daughter? Where is she?"

He stopped, thought, banged his head with his hand. Thought harder. And at last, got an idea.

"Follow me!"

He panted along the long corridors again and down the wide staircase, across the baronial hall and into the dining-room, where, only the day before yesterday, he had broken his teeth on a golden apple and begun to learn his lesson.

There was everything just as he had left it, and the Mumbo goggled. The golden table, the golden objects, the golden food. And the golden dog.

Whipping out the de-spelling fluid, Midas dropped some on Spray's back. In a second he was alive again, jumping up on the King trying to lick his face and barking a frantic welcome-home.

117

Acky-backy arched his back, made a diamond-shaped mouth like a viper, hissed snakily and retreated under the golden cloth.

"Good old boy, good dog!" cried Midas joyfully. And then: "Where's Delia, Stray? Find that girl! Find her!"

Stray took off. He dashed out of the room, with the other three after him.

The dog seemed so full of purpose that the King's hopes rose again. He dashed upstairs to the Princess's bedroom, into her playroom, downstairs again into the conservatory-bathroom, onto the terrace. By that time the King had begun to realise the dog had no more notion where to look for the Princess than he had, but as Stray continued to tear from room to room there seemed nothing for it but to follow, though they were all desperately out of breath.

"I've heard about dogs!" puffed the mumbo, trailing smoke from his chest-fire. "They go by smell! If she's still made of gold, she won't have left a scent . . . he'll never find her!"

Sure enough, after going through all the rooms the Princess usually used, Stray came to a baffled stop. He sank onto his haunches and scratched his ear.

"Can't you talk to him?" asked Midas.

"Me? I've never seen a dog before. I can only speak Cat because I grew up with Acky. It's no use, we'll never find her."

But now it was the King who wouldn't give up. He crouched beside Stray.

118

"Find Biffpot," he ordered slowly and clearly.

Stray cocked his head. He had never been asked this before.

"Stray, old friend, be clever now! Biffpot, Biffpot, you know, my valet?" And as Stray still looked blank, the King lost patience.

"BIFFPOT!" he roared.

They were all electrified by a faint answering shout, like an echo:

"Sire!"

The King leapt up. Stray took off again, as if after a rabbit, yipping with excitement. They followed him. He tore to the back of the palace, and, rounding a corner, they saw him scratching and whining at a green baize door.

"The cellars!"

The King wrenched the door open. Stray streaked down the steps ahead of them.

The palace cellars were quite extensive. They were spread out beneath the whole palace. Some were used for storing wine, others for works of art, and still others for food. It was quite dark but the King was used to the dark by now.

"Mumbo, turn on your luminosity!"

The baby dragon huffed and puffed till he glowed green and red. At the far end of the main central passage they could see Stray, pawing at the base of a door.

They hurried to him. The King tried to open the door, but it was locked from the inside. He put his ear against it and thought he heard a faint sound.

"Are you in there, Biffpot?"

"Is th-that you, Y-your M-majesty?" asked a faint and trembling voice from the other side of the door.

"Biffpot, you blithering idiot! Open this door at once! Do you hear me?" roared the King.

There was a creak as the key slowly turned. The door opened a crack, and by the light of a candle Biffpot's pointed nose and one eye could be seen.

"Has she g-gone, Sire?"

"Gone? Yes, gone, gone, Biffpot! And you let her be stolen!"

"Stolen, Sire? I? Let the witch be stolen?"

"Who's talking about the witch, man? It's my daughter I mean! She has been stolen, and you, who were left to guard her as the most precious treasure in my kingdom, I find skulking down here in hiding while—"

"She is here, Sire!"

The King stopped short in the midst of his tirade. "What!"

"I have Her Highness here with me, Sire, safe and sound, though . . . in rather a peculiar condition, if you will excuse the liberty of a personal remark."

He opened the door all the way, and stood aside.

"Mumbo, stay out of sight," ordered the King.

The room was a little whitewashed larder, filled with smoked hams and chickens, barrels of flour and potatoes and pickled herrings, big chests of tea and rows of jars of jam.

At first the King couldn't see the Princess, but then he saw Biffpot's eyes rolling upward towards the ceiling. The King glanced up – and his jaw dropped.

There she was – just as he had last seen her, still bent over to tuck him into bed, still looking like solid gold – only now she was floating among the strings of herbs and the smoked hams. A piece of rope dangled from her waist.

Slowly and silently the King pulled on the rope and brought her down to the ground. He touched her. She was still made of gold, but, thanks to the witch's spell, at the same time she was lighter than air. He tied the rope to a convenient barrel, and then turned to Biffpot.

"Biffpot, my friend. How can I apologise for my rash words? I have been cured of one curse, but the curse of my quick temper I must still conquer . . . I see it all now. The witch came in my absence, and you – left to face her alone—"

Biffpot shuddered. "Horrible it was, Sire. She came towards the palace like a rocket, making a terrible whirring, fizzling noise. Frightened out of my wits I was. And her face as she burst in through the window! Never saw anything to touch it, Sire. Enough to freeze a man's blood.

"Next thing I know, there I am lying on the floor, and the witch is getting on her broomstick and threatening to be back in two ticks, and

Her Highness bobbing about near the ceiling, Sire!

"So I fetched a rope and a ladder and went up after her. Then I brought her down here. Thinking it was the safest place. Towed her, rather. Extremely awkward it was, Sire, trying not to bump her, and her so buoyant, and yet so – brittle, if you take my meaning, Sire."

"Biffpot," said the King soberly. "I am deeply proud of you. Pray go down on one knee. I am going to make you a Knight."

Biffpot blushed with pleasure and obeyed. The King remembered too late that he hadn't got his sword with him, but rather than spoil the moment he picked up a large ham, and, holding it tight with both hands, touched Biffpot first on one shoulder and then on the other.

"Arise, Sir Biffpot!" he said, mopping his brow. "And now – and now—!"

Carefully and with trembling hands, the King opened the witch's bottle for the third time, dipped his fingers in, and threw a few drops on to Delia's golden curls.

As they watched breathlessly, the deathly gold receded, and in its place her own human colouring returned. For the King, it was almost like watching his sweet queen returning to life – the summery hair, warm tender skin, bright brown eyes opening again on this world, and meeting his own that were spilling tears of joy.

"Oh, my dear darling!" he choked out, clasping her in his arms. "Forgive me! Forgive me!"

"Daddy—"

The King cuddled her close, and knew for certain that he had never been so happy in his life.

Chapter Eleven

Return of the Magician

*T*here were some difficulties about the addition of the mumbo and Acky-backy to the palace household.

Stray and Acky took one look at each other and declared total war. They chased one another from end to end of the palace and all around the grounds, until both fell to the floor in exhaustion. Acky recovered first, and leapt onto a high piece of furniture, from where he gazed down upon the recumbent Stray, waiting for him to be ready for another chase.

Sir Biffpot got the fright of his life – well, almost – when he first saw the mumbo, and refused to come anywhere near him.

"It's a mumbo, Sire! A genuine, live mumbo!" he kept jibbering.

"I know it's a mumbo, Biffpot. A friendly one – a baby one."

"Baby my foot, Sire, if you'll pardon me! I have made quite a little study of dragons and I know what I'm talking about. That is a well-grown *adolescent* mumbo, on the very verge of doing its shoot. A year from now, Sire, you won't recognise it, Sire, its head will be through the roof and its wingspan will stretch from one side of the throne-room to the other! Take my word for it!"

The mumbo preened himself and smirked with pride.

"Not quite that big," he murmured. "Still, I will be gi-normous, I won't deny that."

"AAAAAGH! It talks!" shrieked Biffpot, turning to flee.

The King caught him. "He was stolen at birth and brought up by the witch," he explained soothingly. "She taught him human language."

Biffpot goggled at the King.

"And that won't be all she taught it, I have no doubt! It'll be putting spells on us all next, if it doesn't burn us alive in our beds or make a meal of us!"

The mumbo was sniggering in his rude way at poor Biffpot's antics. "No, I won't, honestly I won't. I never learnt any of her rotten spells. Listen, I *want* to live here with you lot, I'm not likely to do anything that would make you kick me out."

At this moment Delia, who had been watching the mumbo from a doorway, stepped forward. She shook the mumbo's paw without the slightest fear.

"How do you do?" she said politely. "My teacher says there are practically no dragons left, so I think I'm very lucky to meet one."

The King was watching carefully. Would the mumbo find her irresistibly fanciable, and want to cut his new teeth on her? He was certainly sniffing at her, and now the tip of his forked tongue came out and gave her chin a lick. Was he – *tasting* her?

"Mumbo!" Midas said sternly. "That Princess is *not* for eating!"

"Couldn't choke down all that hair, anyway, though I must say ... she is very sweet ..." He ran the tongue around her face, making her giggle. "Hmmm! Almost as superscrumptious as a flandy-bake! I bet she'd taste even better toasted!" And he blew a little puff of smoke into her face.

"You'd better be joking," said the King sternly. "One nibble, just one – and you're out – to face the big, cold, hunter-filled, flandy-bake-less world."

The mumbo sighed gustily, and rested his head on the Princess's shoulder.

"Oh ... All right then," he said. "I won't if you insist. I could only eat her once, after all, and after that I couldn't have her to play with." Delia giggled again and tickled him behind the ear.

It was a very happy party that gathered round the table at lunchtime.

It was a plain wooden table, with a plain

linen cloth. On it were plain china dishes and plain stainless steel knives and forks; plain pewter drinking mugs and a glass bowl of plain red roses. There were wax candles in brass stands, and as much good plain food as anyone could eat.

The King looked round at all this and said, "I wouldn't change one thing for all the gold in the world!" His hand strayed to the locket at his neck, and he thought, *This holds the only gold that I need for the rest of my life.*

Sir Biffpot and Midas between them had made the lunch. Luckily Biffpot had once been a cook-general. It was some time since the King had visited his kitchens, and he was surprised by how much he enjoyed cooking.

"We'll have to engage a whole new staff," he said to Biffpot. "But perhaps we'll manage on fewer servants, Biffpot, what do you think? It's time I stopped wasting my life and took more interest in things. *Real* things."

"You've always taken a great interest in the roses, Sire."

"The roses ... Ah well, that's different." Fleetingly he thought of the Midas rose, his great creation, now lost, but after all, he could start work on a new one – a yellow one, perhaps. No. No. Not yellow! Too like gold. A white one, then. Or a striped one. Ever since he'd seen the flandy-bakes he'd had the idea of a rose striped pink and white like them.

Delia sat between the King and the mumbo. She ate heartily, even tasting a flandy-bake, though she didn't like them as much as chocolate biscuits.

"Where's Mumbo going to live, Daddy?"

"Well, I thought the conservatory."

"You mean – my bathroom?"

"Yes, darling. There's nowhere else for him, really. It's nice and warm in there, and there's plenty of room for him to grow."

Biffpot shook his head gloomily. "Won't hold him, Sire. Another six months—"

"I'll have it enlarged, then!"

"The flandy-bakes will grow well in there I expect," said the mumbo. "I'm going to plant lots of them in separate pots."

"Good idea! A whole orchard of them! I wonder if you could cross a flandy-bake with a rose," mused the King.

"But what about my bath?" asked the Princess.

"You can still use the pool for your bath, my love, I'm sure the mumbo won't mind."

"He'll have to turn his back," Delia said primly.

Speaking of backs reminded her of something she'd been thinking of ever since she saw the mumbo.

"When you're full-grown and can fly," she said, "could I have a ride on you?"

"Yes," said the mumbo.

"No!" said the King at the same time. "Nobody is going to fly away with my girl!" Everyone laughed. Except Midas. He wasn't laughing.

* * *

After lunch the King went round the palace by himself, quietly turning everything that had been gold back into its proper form. When he'd done that, he went out into the garden and did the same there, sprinkling the purple fluid over roses and statues, trees and stones, and even the gardener's spade.

At last he came to his golden jacket, lying stiffly in the grass, and when he had changed that back to its old tweed self and put it on, it felt like the arm of an old friend around his shoulders.

Then he went to stand by the place where the Midas bush had grown, and quietly and solemnly said:

"Red rose, bloom again!"

There was a sound like somebody whistling. The King looked round quickly, and there was the little old magician himself, blowing one of his black cigars as if it were a flute, and producing a very jolly tune.

"Hallo," said the King.

The old magician stopped playing and looked up, starting as if in great surprise.

"Back already?" he said. "Find Old Gollop, did you?"

"Yes, no thanks to you," said the King.

"Couldn't help it if I got called away, could I?" asked Nandan.

"I think that was one of your tricks, to make me think out everything for myself," said Midas shrewdly.

"One of my *tricks*!" echoed the old man peevishly. "Do you take me for a common conjuror?" He threw the cigar-flute down. The sound it made on hitting the ground was like a discordant blast on five different brass instruments.

"Please don't be angry," begged the King. "Everything's wonderful now."

"'No thanks to me' I suppose," mimicked the old man, still annoyed. "Going to say the whole thing's my fault, I wouldn't wonder! Who taught you the meaning of real happiness, eh? Eh?"

"You did," said the King, eager to put him in a good temper again. A picture came to him of Delia, grown into a tall and beautiful young woman, standing in her wedding dress beside this two-foot-high little man with a beard right to the ground and wrinkles all over his face . . .

As if reading his thoughts, the magician snapped: "Shouldn't be a bit surprised if you told me I hadn't earned my reward!"

"Oh, you've earned it all right," said the King gloomily. "Only you won't forget the proviso?"

"The proviso? You mean, that I can't have her unless she wants me? And you don't think she will want an old fellow like me, eh?" He lifted his beard on both withered hands and stared at it. "It's a possibility . . . a distinct possibility," he said, and now he, too, sounded gloomy. "Ah . . . If only Wuzzleflump—"

"You knew the witch?" asked the King interestedly.

Nandan dropped his beard. "Did you run into her, by any chance?"

"I did, indeed! She's 'no more', you know."

The magician's face went suddenly white. "You mean—?"

"Yes. And I was the one who – er – well, at any rate, I happen to know she's no more."

He somehow thought Nandan would be pleased about this, but instead the old man threw his hands upward, turned his face to the sky and let out a howl of despair.

"No More! No More! My last hope – gone for ever!" he wailed.

"What on earth do you mean?" asked the King anxiously.

"Oh, how could you, of all people, bring me such terrible news!"

"But why is it terrible?"

"How did it happen?"

"She was such a mass of spells and witchcraft and black magic that when the Cijam water touched her, she – just seemed to—"

Abruptly the magician leapt into the air, grasped the King by the lapels and brought him down till they were facing each other nose to nose.

"Tell me! Tell me quickly! How did you get unmagicked? Was it anything to do with *her*?"

"No, no. It was the Cijam water, just as you advised."

"No good, no good! Tried it many times. Not strong enough. *Her* spells are so much stronger than mine. She was a mistress of her craft, one of the most powerful witches in the world . . . Only one of her own antidotes could possibly work on me . . ."

And, out of sheer misery it seemed, the old man started to melt as before.

"Well, I do have a few drops left," said the King doubtfully.

Nandan stopped melting. He looked very funny, partly melted, but the King didn't laugh.

"A flew drlops . . . ?" he slurred in his syrupy, melting voice.

"Yes. Of this purply stuff the mumbo and I found left over in her cauldron. It restored everything I'd touched."

Nandan sprang back into his complete unmelted self. His white eyebrows bristled, his hair stood on end. Even the Midas rose seemed to stiffen on his chest. Every inch of him was alert.

"Show me! Quickly!"

The King fished out the nearly-empty bottle.

"Ah-h-h!" breathed Nandan, and his bright eyes became brighter than ever. "I wonder . . . Could it be . . . ? Can I have that?"

"Er – well . . ."

"What? You hesitate?"

"It seems to be very important to you. Of course, you may have it, but . . ."

"BUT WHAT?"

"My rose was very important to me. If I could just have the bush back . . . no blooms . . . so it will flower next year . . ."

"You drive a hard bargain, Midas!"

"I learnt the skill from you," said the King.

"Done!" He made a swift gesture, and the Midas bush, empty of flowers, appeared in its old place. "Now, quickly! The antidote!"

The King handed over the bottle. The old man snatched it, held it to the light, squinted through it, sniffed it, and at last shook one of the last drops onto his finger and carried it to his lips.

"Oh, I shouldn't *eat* it!" said the King anxiously.

"You never know," said the magician, and sucked the liquid off his finger.

The King waited breathlessly for some violent change to come over him, but apart from the slow, satisfied smile that spread over his face, the little old man remained exactly the same.

"Now," he said, "all we need is . . . Ah!"

The King heard Delia calling him, and then saw her running towards him from the palace. She had something cupped in her hands, and her feet skimmed over the grass as lightly as a shadow.

"Daddy!" she called. "Daddy, you forgot – oh!" She stopped short on seeing the little magician, who was standing with feet apart and hands behind his back, his eyebrows beetling towards her and a very strange expression – half tender, half anxious – on his face.

For a moment the Princess and Nandan stared at each other.

"Hallo," he said at last.

"Hallo," she answered shyly. Then she turned

134

to the King. "Daddy," she said anxiously. "You forgot to bring my little bird back to life!" And she showed him the tiny golden figure in her hands.

"So I did!" said the King in dismay. "And now I've given this gentleman what's left of the magic charm. You must ask him very nicely if he's got a drop to spare for your bird."

The Princess turned to the magician, but before she could speak, he bowed almost to the ground like a grand courtier.

"You need not ask me, gentle young lady," he said. "It will be my pleasure to oblige you." And he handed her the bottle with the last of the witch's brew inside.

"Oh, thank you, that is kind of you!" She gave his wrinkled cheek a kiss, and, forgetting the grown-ups, sat down at once cross-legged on the grass with the bottle in her hand and the bird in her lap, intent on bringing it back to life.

"Well, well, well," said Nandan slowly. "So small a thing . . . a kiss . . . so small a thing, to work so great a miracle."

The Princess was so preoccupied with the bird that she didn't see what happened next. But the King was watching. At first he couldn't believe his eyes. The old man, who was stroking his beard as he often did, suddenly gave it an extra sharp tug – and it came right off in his hand!

And that was just the beginning.

He threw the beard into the air, and it shrivelled up and disappeared. Underneath, the King

saw that his chin was young and strong, and . . .
was it his imagination, or had the wrinkles above
disappeared as well?

The little man, seeming not to notice the
King's stare, yawned and stretched his arms as
if waking from a deep sleep. As he stretched, he
grew taller and taller until – until the King found
himself looking UP into those twinkling eyes!

Then, in the middle of his stretch, the magician rubbed both hands through his grey hair,
and afterwards it wasn't grey at all, but brown
and glossy as a horse-chestnut.

When he had finished stretching, he had
turned into a strapping, handsome young man,
looking no more than twenty years old.

"H-how did you do that?" gasped the King in
amazement.

"Shhh!" Nandan put his fingers to his lips and
pointed to the Princess, who was still busy with
the little bird and had not noticed anything. Then
he leant over and whispered in the King's ear:

"I annoyed the witch one day – several centu-
ries ago – by clearing Old Gollop's throat when
she'd blocked it, and she caught me unawares
and turned me into an old man. For years I've
searched for the antidote, but the closest I came
was a description in an old book of magic: 'a
purple potion for the curing of all visible bodily
spells', plus, for my particular one, a young girl's
unasked kiss."

"I see!" said the King, rather dazed.

The young magician looked for a moment at

the shining golden head of the Princess. "Well, I must be on my way."

"Before you go," said the King, "I'd just like to know why you went to the trouble of giving me my wish and teaching me about happiness."

"I attended her birth," said Nandan slowly. "I watched, powerless against the forces of death, as her mother died. Believe me, I tried my best, but I am only a young magician – my powers have not increased since my transformation. But I saw to it that into this little one passed all the beauty and goodness of that dear woman, your queen.

"And I loved the child. I've loved her all her life. I shall love her as long as she lives, which, as I study more now the spell is off me, I can assure you will be long. But I am not a prince. Even my magic can't produce a more beautiful rose than the Midas." He bent his curly head to smell the King's rose, still fastened to his waistcoat. "So I knew I'd have to use – forgive me – just a little magic to marry your daughter."

At this moment, the Princess looked up.

"Look, Daddy! Isn't he pretty now he's alive again?"

The little bird was perched on her finger. It opened its throat on a song of joy.

"Yes, my darling," said the King, helping her to her feet.

"Did that nice little man go away?" asked Delia, looking round.

The King, too, looked round. The place where the young man had stood was empty; but a voice

138

in his ear whispered: "In seven years' time!" and the King thought he saw the ghost of a red rose hover in the air for a moment.

"Yes, he's gone."

The Princess stroked the bird gently with one finger. "Do you think he'll ever come back to visit us?"

"He'll come back all right," said the King, with just a touch of sadness. He put his arm round his daughter.

"Good," she said. "I liked him. I liked his twinkly eyes. But I love you best," she said, and pulled his head down for a kiss.

The King smiled and sighed, both at the same time. Then he saw Stray racing towards them, and feeling suddenly and completely himself again, he said:

"Let's just stroll round to the greenhouse and see how the mumbo's settling in."

And the three of them walked away together over the smiling lawns, with the small, reborn bird singing on Delia's finger.